Captive

Book 1 in the New Life Series

Samantha Jacobey

Lavish Publishing, LLC ~ Houston

Samantha Jacobey

Copyright

2014 Lavish Publishing, LLC eBook edition

Copyright © 2013

Previously Published as: *A New Life – Life of Recovery*

All Rights Reserved

Published in the United States by Lavish Publishing, LLC, Houston

Cover Design by: Nicolene Lorette Design

ISBN 13: 978-0692024355

ISBN 10: 0692024352

www.LavishPublishing.com

Edition, License Note

Table of Contents

Sneak Peek of Bound

Awakening

Tori lay still, the darkness crashing in around her. She could hear voices, muffled and tense. A slow rhythmical BEEP was beginning to break through the blackness, seeping into her clouded mind. BEEP . . . BEEP . . . BEEP. The air was cold to breathe. BEEP . . . BEEP . . . BEEP .The smell was strange, unfamiliar. The voices, all male, rose and fell, as if in the midst of a quiet, yet heated discussion.

Eddie? No—it couldn't be Eddie. Eddie is dead. BEEP . . . BEEP . . . BEEP. The soft hum of machines was becoming noticeable. Warm blankets felt heavy lying across her body. BEEP . . . BEEP . . . BEEP. Does she dare move? *Where is this place? Am I dead?* The first coherent thoughts formed. *Lie still.* Tori's instincts kicked in. *You mustn't draw attention—not yet.*

"Sir, I think she may be regaining consciousness." A woman's voice spoke. Tori didn't like women. Well, the fact was, she really didn't know any. As the hum of the machines continued, she focused on the beeping. Constant . . . Slow . . . Even . . . Pulsing . . . BEEP . . . BEEP . . . BEEP. She could hear the men's voices becoming less muffled, closer now, as if within reach.

Keeping her eyes closed, she lay still and listened, focused on taking deep steady breaths. She was hoping to find clues to her location, and maybe a glimpse of how she got there. The voices rumbled on, only small fragments making sense . . . "I am telling you this girl knows what happened in that house—" (another man's voice cut in) "—and I am telling you it is unlikely we will get anything useful out of her . . ." Tori blinked, unable to control the action. "That's enough you two—she does appear to be rejoining the living," a third male voice directed with an authoritative tone.

Silence followed, broken only by the steady

beep and hum of the equipment around her. Slowly, cautiously; Tori allowed her eyes to open and stare blankly at the ceiling. She could see small, round, very dim lights in the drop-ceiling above her. The tiles were square, with the typical white foam spongy pattern. She could hear the breathing of the three men as they stood close to her now.

The man to her right had a raspy breath, huffing a bit more heavily than the others. Tori guessed he was a fat man, but did not dare shift her eyes to check. Lying as if she were made of stone, she stared at the ceiling, willing it to tell her what she needed to know.

How did I get here? Who are these men? What do they want with me? Slowly her mind sifted through the words they had spoken . . . *the house. They know about the house. Yes. The alcohol—it must not have been enough. A hospital. I am lying in a hospital.* Her thoughts were becoming clearer now, and she felt the need to test her situation.

Quick, silent motion, Tori sat straight up, grabbing the front of the man to her right, clenching his tie and using it to pull him off balance towards the bed rail. Reacting just as quickly, the other two men reached out, grasping her hands and pulling their comrade free of her clutches.

Pushing her back down onto the bed, one of them spewing a mix of threats and obscenities, they managed to subdue her in her weakened state. Pain stabbed and throbbed in her left arm as Tori realized she had some type of tubing connected to her. She had no real experience with hospitals, and knew she was at a distinct disadvantage. As she lay pressed into the mattress beneath her, she now cut her eyes to look at the leader of the group. He was indeed a fat man, with a round face, now red from their struggle.

"Just relax," one of the men soothed. "My name is Eli Founder. No one here is going to harm you." He had positioned himself above her, hands pushing down firmly on her shoulders so that he could look her square in the face. He paused for several minutes, waiting for her breathing to slow to normal. Then, he continued, "Can you tell me your name?"

"My name?" Tori spoke the words just above a whisper, her thoughts running wild, *they don't know who I am?*

Eli nodded, "You were naked when you were found, with no ID." He stared down into her eyes, waiting patiently for her answer. He noticed they were crystal blue, and for a moment he thought they looked like deep pools that would swallow him if he were to fall in.

"They call me Tori," she stammered, unsure how to explain or elaborate any further. He was close enough she could smell the gel in his smooth coal black hair.

"Tori, that's good," Eli half smiled. "That matches an ID that was found in the house and believed to belong to you. Tori Farrell." She cringed as he spoke. The scar that crossed her left eye felt heavy with him staring at it. Slowly, the pressure from his hands eased as he spoke in a low, even tone, "I am going to let go now, but you mustn't struggle. No one wants to hurt you. We're here to help."

Tori could feel the hands release as he pulled away from her, but she did not make another move. Lying still, she allowed her eyes to flit around to each of the men, trying to get a grasp on the moment. The one she had grappled with was straightening his tie and trying to smooth his crumpled suit. He was shorter than the others, weaker. He would have gone down easy if not for his friends.

The third man was the tallest, with dark hair and squinty eyes. "Who are you guys?" she finally asked. Again, Eli spoke in his low, patronizing voice, "I am Special Agent Eli Founder. This gentleman," he indicated the tall man, "This is my partner, Special Agent Warren La Buff."

The fat man quickly spoke up, his tone sharp, "I'm not really important right now. I will leave you two to it." He gave his fellow agents a quick nod as he made a hasty exit from the barren chamber.

Tori was left staring at the remaining men in wonder and disbelief. She was again surrounded by the constant steady beep of the machines and could see that she was bound to them by a series of wires and tubes. Although the two men shared the cramped space, she knew she was more alone now than she had ever been before.

Tori lay silently in the hospital bed, staring at the two men in suits, waiting for them to begin. The room was chill, which made her conscious of her flimsy clinic attire, and she felt grateful for the blankets that warmed her and hid what lay beneath. Patiently she waited, wondering what they knew about her if they knew what her life had been, if they had seen the scars that told the story she was loath to share. If they were waiting for the silence to unnerve her, they would have a long wait. Tori was accustomed to discomfort, and it was the things most people would call normal that scared her most.

Finally, Eli spoke in a soft, comforting voice, "OK Tori, we understand you have been through quite an ordeal, but it is time for you to share what you know with us. It's important you tell us everything you can remember. Let's start with your name. We noticed that there were two men in the house also named Farrell, Edward and

Gerald. Are you in some way related to either or both of those men? Please, tell us anything you can remember about them."

Tori lay silent for several minutes, considering what she knew about Eddie and Red, as they were better known, Farrell. She had known the two men as long as she could remember. As her thoughts turned and skimmed through her memories, she realized the word known was not nearly adequate to describe their relationship. Eddie had called her his most prized possession, and it was a fact that, in many ways, he had owned her, using her as he had pleased, bending her to his will. Finally, she found a small, seemingly safe detail she could share. "Eddie and Red were brothers."

"Yes, identical twins," Eli responded with a small nod, "and their relationship to you?" He noticed she said they *were* brothers, not *are* brothers, *so she is aware that they are dead*.

Again, Tori took her time, searching for the right words. As her mind wandered, it occurred to her that she had not spoken to anyone other than the Dragons in a very long time, years in fact. Not since Eddie had given her the scar that crossed her left eye, the one intended to keep strangers at bay. "Eddie claimed to be my father," was her eventual reply.

The tall agent, La Buff, was stone faced, almost angry in expression, waiting for his moment to pounce on the conversation. Eli agreed that her response was logical, "but why would you say he claimed to be?" And just like that, they had arrived at the parts Tori would give anything not to talk about.

She remained silent, blinking slowly. She allowed her mind to sift through the years she had spent with Eddie Farrell. She had spent her whole life with him and the other Dragons. They had taught her everything they knew, and that is why she had eventually broken free, because they had built her to be strong.

Eventually, La Buff could wait no longer, his biting words cutting through the chill, "You can lay there and blink all you want—we know what happened in that house, and we know what you did to those men." Eli instantly stiffened, turning his head sharply to stare at his partner. Tori was less shocked by his scathing torrent and welcomed the freedom his words afforded her. The truth was already out, and she had nothing to fear in claiming it.

"You found my knife then, I take it?" inside she allowed herself a small sigh of relief, but on the outside her features remained placid.

"We did," La Buff barked.

"Good," Tori's voice stronger now, her confidence growing, "then you should know it was Eddie who gave me that knife. Had my name engraved in it and taught me how to use it very well. I spent my whole life with them, long as I can remember. In the end, I used what they taught me against them, and they got what they deserved."

With that, Tori closed her eyes, and her chest began to rise and fall in deep, steady waves of comfort. She had known pain, and there was nothing they could do to her that had not been done before. The conversation was over, whether the men in suits liked it or not.

First Meeting

As Eli Founder left the hospital room, he could feel the anger welling inside him. Warren La Buff walked smugly beside him, pleased he had put his foot down during the interrogation. "How could you do that?" Founder erupted furiously. "How could you stand there and speak to her that way knowing what the committee has decided?"

"I never agreed with what the committee decided," La Buff answered flatly, then turned sharply into the stairwell and allowed the door to close behind him.

Eli stood stunned for a moment at his partner's hasty exit, briefly considering a pursuit to continue the argument. Thinking better of it, he headed towards the vending machines in the waiting room. As he walked, Eli thought about the meeting that had taken place just one short day before, and the events that had lead up to it.

Things had been fairly chaotic since the discovery of eleven dead men in a farmhouse, but they were not directly the reason for the meeting. The committee was called together to discuss the other body found in the house—that of a girl. Dropping in a few coins, he chose his cup of java, while he appraised the events of the last twenty-four hours.

Agent Founder had not been privy to any details prior to the meeting. As they had entered the conference room, everyone's mood had seemed eerily somber, and at the time he was unclear as to exactly how he and his partner had drawn this assignment. Everyone took their seats, and he noticed that some of the participants were not actually agents at all.

Special Agent James Godfry, head of their division, would preside over the meeting and called everyone to order with his usual throat clearing and a wave of his hand. A short, heavy man, James Godfry had been with the bureau almost three decades and had seen many things, too many things he sometimes suspected. But this case took even him by surprise.

"Good morning everyone, and thank you all for being here on such short notice," Godfry began to read from the case file in his deep, round voice. "Before we begin, I must inform and or remind everyone that everything that is discussed here today is classified top secret in the interests of national security. Although some details have become the knowledge of parties outside of this committee, they have likewise been instructed not to discuss the matter with anyone. This committee is being formed to oversee and conduct an investigation into the incident that occurred in Iowa two days ago. We will evaluate its connection to the investigation code named Castleford."

Immediately, Eli's heart rate jumped at the name of the ugliest case he had ever been involved in, a case that had cost him a partner by the time it was over. Shifting anxiously in his seat, he listened closely as Special Agent Godfry continued. "As far as background, the Castleford case was moved to the cold case files three years ago after an Agent working on the investigation was murdered and all leads basically evaporated. Allow me to give you details on the current situation, and then we will discuss the connection between the two."

"Two days ago, at about 11 pm local time, a farmer in Iowa called the local sheriff's office to report that a group of roughly a dozen hooligans on motorcycles had invaded his neighbor's house—a neighbor he knew to be out of town and not expected to return for several days. The sheriff chose to wait until the next morning before taking action. Shortly after sunrise, he and his three deputies moved in, hoping the crew had moved on ahead of them. When they arrived at the scene, they discovered that the group had, in fact, not moved on, and upon entering the residence discovered an extremely gruesome scene. They found the bodies of eleven men and one woman." Here, Godfry gave pause to allow everyone to process the information before continuing.

"Upon quick inspection, the sheriff and his men noted that all of the men were, in fact, deceased and that the female, although alive, was barely so, and had her quickly transported to the local hospital where she was treated for severe alcohol poisoning. After being stabilized, she was placed in ICU under police supervision, and we were contacted." Again, Godfry gave a brief pause as several of the attendees began to shift in their chairs as they listened.

"Once we were apprised of the situation, we had the still unconscious female transferred to one of the Mercy Hospital affiliates here in Chicago, where we have kept her sedated until we are ready to question her as to her involvement in and knowledge of the events that occurred in Iowa two days ago."

At this pause, a gentleman to Godfry's right cleared his throat and took the opportunity to put forth a question, "so what does this have to do with Castleford?"

"Maybe nothing," Godfry stated matter-of-factly, "Maybe everything. Two of the bodies found in the house where directly named in the Castleford investigation. That is why this committee has been formed—to deal with the girl and use her to get some answers if at all possible."

Eli decided it was time for him to speak up, "So what exactly does, 'deal with the girl' mean? Is she a witness? Is she a surviving victim? Is she the perpetrator of the murders? I mean, what are we looking at here?"

"Those are all very good questions," praised Godfry, "and we will be working within this group to determine all of those things. We will not do so in a short amount of time by any means. This is going to take some time to sort out. Right now, I feel it might be more beneficial to hear from Dr. Bennet. If you would please sir, give us your evaluation of this young woman and her standing in this situation."

"Well, firstly, I am not sure I would call her a woman," began Dr. Bennet, "This girl has been thoroughly examined and after considering several factors, I can strongly conclude that she is no more than 15 years of age, probably less, and has one of the most severely battered bodies that I have ever seen." He didn't look at Special Agent Godfry as he rendered his assessment, knowing this would be the grounds they would use to control the young woman if need be.

"We have determined that she had relations of a sexual nature with at least 5 of the deceased men on the night in question, and her body shows signs of several years of sexual and physical abuse." He referred to the reports before him, adding to his credibility, "That being said, it is currently difficult to determine if she was, in fact, a victim or an aggressor in this instance. Since we have evidence going both ways, we just don't know."

"So what you are saying is, she could be a victim, but she could be one of the bad guys," Eli clarified giving him a thumbs up as he spoke, and the doctor nodded his agreement. "Ok," Eli continued, "So who is she?"

"We don't know that either," Godfry interjected, "There was an ID in the house with her picture on it, completely fake, and so far we have come up empty on every database at our disposal. Oddly enough, every man killed was easily identified through military records, which makes it even odder with regards to what she was doing there with them and why she alone survived."

Godfry studied his subordinate for a moment, then clarified the situation, "So, this is what we are going to do. We are going to pump this girl for every drop we can get from her, hope it leads us to some answers here on this case and gets us back on track with Castleford. That means you two," he pointed at Founder and La Buff, "are going to go play nice, see what you can find out."

"But she is going to prison," La Buff spoke up, "if she is found to have been involved, she will be prosecuted, correct?"

Godfry hesitated, leaning back in his chair to consider his words carefully, "I realize that under normal circumstances, anyone found in a house full of bodies would become the primary suspect with prosecution as a forgone conclusion. However, these are not normal circumstances.

This young lady presents a large number of problems as well as opportunities for us, and so this matter needs to be handled delicately. I would go easy on the prison talk. She is pretty banged up, and it would be mighty tough to get a jury to convict even if we could show she had a hand in the deed. I think we can all pretty well agree, it is in our best interest to tread lightly and see what we can get from her."

"See what we can get from her," Eli repeated blankly. "And how do you propose we go about doing that? I mean; it would go a lot smoother if she wanted to tell us what she knows."

"Yes. Yes, it would." Godfry agreed, "And fortunately we have a plan for that. Dr. Bennet, would you care to explain?" And so Dr. Andrew Bennet explained how they intended to make Tori believe she is helping herself by telling them what they needed to know.

Eli nodded as he listened, ready to do his part and pretty much whatever it takes to get the person or people responsible for his former partner's death. Giving his current partner a sideways glance, he doubted Warren La Buff was as enthusiastic.

Recovery

It seemed like days that Tori spent recovering in the tiny room. Nurses would come in and out, checking her tubes and wires, and eventually removing them. One nurse with 'Jane' on her name badge outlined the rules for her. She could get out of bed and walk around if she felt strong enough. Do not leave the room. The bathroom is behind this tiny door. Pull this string if you need help when you are in there. Here are some fresh gowns and towels. Take a shower if you feel like it.

If I feel like it? Tori's thoughts raced with excitement. She had spent most of her life dirty and ragged, covered in grease and the grime of men. Showers were like her ultimate reward, the one treat she was rarely given and craved the most. She would do anything for the feel of warm water and the chance to be clean, even if only for a few hours.

As soon as the woman left her, Tori slipped into the tiny bathroom, dropping the gown to the floor and turning on the shower. As she stepped beneath the warm spray, a loud gleeful gasp escaped her, and she ran her hands over her bare skin, tracing the path of the water.

After a few minutes of standing with the cascade splashing down on her upturned face, she found the soap contained in a strange pump bottle. It had an odd fruity smell, but it made large bubbles as she rubbed it across her sticky flesh, and she felt the tense lines in her face soften with the pleasure of lathering and rinsing her delicate female parts.

Finally, she put her forehead against the wall, allowing the water to pour onto her clean hair and wash down her back. A small trickle found its way over her front and followed the curve and plunge between her breasts. She used a finger to trace the rounded scar that hugged the inside of her left breast, squarely between the nipple and breast bone.

It was a bite mark Eddie had given her years ago. He had laughed about it at the time and said, "Now you will never forget your place." Tori would often place her hand over that spot whenever she felt the temptation to disobey him, and she almost never forgot her place.

Her fingers wrinkled; she grew tired of the water and shut off the valve. As she ran the towel over her other scars, she thought about how each had been acquired, or at least the ones she had been sober enough to remember.

Eventually, her thoughts landed on Henry. Henry Morgan, the only Dragon to show Tori any measure of kindness. He was the one who held her close to keep her warm when she was young. He was the one who brushed her long black mane and taught her how to care for herself whenever she had the chance. The one who made her feel special; the only one she had ever thought of as a friend.

Henry had told Tori that one day she would have a different life. She had dismissed the thought—a foolish waste of time to even hope for such a thing. Now, standing in that tiny hospital bathroom, it looked as if her friend and mentor might have been right.

Henry had been gone six months now. Eddie had killed him after an argument. Tori had never been sure what the fight had been about. She only knew it had angered Eddie to the point of killing one of their own, so it must have been something very bad. She had missed the old fool terribly though and had grown more contemptuous each day since his passing. In a way, it was his death that finally gave her the strength to do what had to be done.

Tori looked around the small chamber. After her shower, she was feeling comfortable and a bit restless with a need to explore. The walls were stark white, with no decorations, but an outline on the wall next to the bed hinted a painting of some kind had hung there at one time. In the far left corner, opposite the door, there stood a plain wooden chair. Tori considered sitting in it briefly before opting to rummage through the few cabinets that surrounded the small sink on the wall opposite the bed.

However, the search proved fruitless, as every cupboard was bare, and she was again left to choose between the bed and the chair. After a moment, she opted for neither. Tori dropped to her knees in the empty corner of the room where she would be hidden from view by anyone entering through the wide door. This was a typical location for her, corners and hidden spots, and she felt much more relaxed as she squatted down with her shoulder leaning into the corner, and her face pressed into the cool paint of the wall. Within minutes, she was fast asleep.

Tori spent three days cowering in the corner of her room before it was decided to move her. During that time, she had only one visitor—Eli Founder. He would come to the room each morning before breakfast thinking he would get there before she awoke, and catch her sleeping in the bed. Instead, he always found her awake and wide eyed, crouched in the far corner of the room, listening to the silence. So, he would sit in the hard wooden chair facing her and make small talk, mostly with himself.

By the third day, he had come to realize this girl was unlike any he had ever, or probably would ever, meet. Her answers to questions always seemed honest, but were never rushed or elaborate. Her face was the most expressionless he had ever seen, almost as if it were made of china like a doll. He noted her hair was long and thick, reaching the small of her back in black waves, while her eyes like crystal blue spheres, staring into eternity.

She would sit with her back against the wall and her right shoulder pressed into the corner. She kept her knees pulled up to her chest, with her arms wrapped tightly around them, resting her cheek on the top of them, so that her face was only half exposed at a time. It was during one of these sessions Eli noticed how strikingly beautiful she was, at least half of her was, when the scar was covered, and all that could be seen was the right side of her face.

"Where did you go to school?" Eli asked.

After an appropriate length of silence, "I never went to school," came the reply.

"Can you read and write?" another question, followed by a long silence and "of course," being the short and simple response.

When asking questions did not seem to be getting him anywhere, Eli decided to tell her stories about his life in hopes of drawing her out to share her own. In the end, he shared a great deal about himself, while she sat in calm indifference, and shared nothing of her own life. By the end of the third day, he was completely at a loss. He knew something was going to have to change if he were to have any hope of reopening Castleford.

It was on that day that Warren La Buff entered the room with two other men dressed in white. He laid a white uniform on the bed, instructed Eli to be sure she changed promptly, and then the three of them stepped back outside. Eli picked up the uniform and inspected it briefly before returning it to the bed.

Turning towards Tori, he nodded, "go ahead. I will find out what's going on while you get dressed." As he headed out the door himself, the thought occurred to him how protective of her he had come to feel, as though she were in his charge.

"What's going on?" he demanded of his partner. "I thought you wanted off this case."

"I do," La Buff bit a stiff reply, "But the powers that might be won't allow it. So, we are stuck, babysitting, until this is wrapped up, and she is either committed long term or set free. Me? I would rather see her committed, but at this point, I don't really care as long as I get to move on to more important cases."

"You're such a pig," Eli replied, his voice dripping with contempt. "Three years you have been my partner, and I never realized how much I despise you until now."

The two men stood in angry silence waiting for Tori to emerge. After several minutes, Eli decided to check on her and rapped lightly on the door before peeking inside. She stood in her corner wearing the new clothes, patiently waiting for the next command. She turned her face towards him as he entered her expression a blank stare; he managed a smile and a cheerful, "are you ready?"

In compliance, Tori stepped towards the door, her hands folded in front of her. Outside, she looked perfectly cool, lethargic even. Inside, her heart pounded, and her mind raced. *Where are we going? Is this my chance to escape? Should I escape?* When she stepped up beside him, she could see Eli glance down at her hands and instinctively she knew he was considering cuffing her.

Slowly, she raised her hands, offering them to him like a sacrifice. Cuffs meant there would be no escape. Not in unfamiliar territory, with no weapons or tools. Besides, attempting to escape could mean hurting him, and even though she was not particularly fond of him, she had never harmed anyone without orders, except for the Dragons of course.

Eli Founder had been kind to her, the first man since Henry to treat her with respect. No, she wasn't particularly fond of him, but she needed him somehow, and would have done anything he asked of her to prove it.

A Room with a View

After securing the cuffs about her wrists, Eli led Tori out of her hospital room. They followed Warren La Buff down the hallway towards the elevators, the two men in white uniforms bringing up the rear. Eli had placed his hand on her elbow to guide her, so Tori felt free to take in her surroundings as they moved.

The walls were white, but the rooms they passed seemed cheerier, having cushioned couches and paintings to decorate the walls. As they walked, she peered into more open doors, enough to know for certain her room had been stripped just for her. *How did they know I would sit on the empty floor?* She pondered their motives as they shuffled onto the elevator, still allowing her new friend to guide her.

Once they had reached the ground floor, the group marched out onto a patio containing a trolley cart of sorts. La Buff grabbed Tori's free arm and pushed on her back to direct her to climb aboard; his touch shocked her, and her reaction was swift.

Twisting her upper body, Tori pulled her arm free and stepped away, a sharp yelping noise escaping her. Eli intervened, waiving his partner away while turning to face the girl as if to ask what was wrong.

The girl stopped moving, taking in a deep breath and allowing it to escape through tightly clenched teeth. "I don't like to be touched," she stated flatly. She stood for a moment, staring into his eyes while Eli evaluated her statement, aware that he had been touching her ever since they had left her room.

Shifting aside, he allowed her to move into the cart and choose a seat, and then sat down beside her. Once everyone was aboard, one of the white uniforms drove them along the path. As they moved, the shadow of the trees along the left side passed across their faces, alternating with the glow of the sun, and Tori was able to get her bearings for the first time since her arrival.

They rode for several minutes before she noticed Eli was watching her intently. When she turned to stare at him, he gave her a quick smile and nod of his head. "I think you are going to like this place," he said in a low voice, leaning closer so she could hear him over the noise of the vehicle.

Eventually, they turned a corner and arrived at a large pair of glass doors. The cart lumbered to a stop, and the group exited the transport to make their way inside. The lobby was stunning, with the sun shining in through the walls and roof made of paned glass, the light pouring down onto a large fountain and pond area surrounded by small trees, with hanging vines clinging to their limbs.

The sight took her breath away, and for a moment Tori remained still and closed her eyes to listen. The sound of the running water lifted her away, and for a split second, she was sitting on the bank of a small waterway the Dragons had frequented when she was a child. In that instant, Henry was alive and sitting beside her, and Tori could almost feel the warmth of his presence as he brushed her long hair. A stab of loneliness pierced her soul as she opened her eyes to the beautiful sight before her, knowing Henry was not really there to share it with her.

Again the group moved forward, turning down a long hallway to the right, following it when it made a turn to the left. Three doors down on the left, Warren La Buff stopped and turned into the room that had been prepared for her. For a second time, the walls were plain, and the furniture simple. Looking in, Tori could see that there were two padded chairs on either side of a small round table on the far side of the room. Directly behind the table and chairs was a small, square, multi-paned window that looked out onto a well-tended garden path.

Tori made her way into the area, where she noticed the bathroom was set off to the right just as you entered the chamber, and a small closet space and built-in dresser stood on the left. Inwardly, Tori felt a small pang of amusement, knowing that all of the clothes she owned would not fill a single drawer.

Moving beyond the narrow entry hall formed by the bathroom and closet area, she could see the twin bed on the right, running along the wall connected to the bathroom. It was positioned so that if you lay on the bed, you could see straight out the window and into the garden area, or you could close the small white curtains that hung to the sides of the window to hide the view.

Leaning back and gazing out into and across the hallway, Tori could view the room on the other side of the hall. Directly in line, she could see the bed running along the left hand wall, just as it had been in all the other rooms she had passed.

Realizing that she had noticed the change, Eli shrugged and explained with a small smile, "Maybe you will feel more comfortable sleeping in the bed if it is in a more protected location."

Tori felt touched that he had noticed her

need to hide, and felt a stab of loyalty towards the man standing beside her. She knew it would be difficult to sleep in the bed, but for him, she would at least try. Holding up her cuffed wrists, she stared into his cool grey eyes as he removed her shiny bonds; her porcelain expression unmoved.

After the room had cleared, Tori turned and sat on the bed to stare at the dresser. Her mind began to wander, and she thought about the old backpack she used to carry her change of clothes and personal items in when the Dragons were on the road. Well, they were always on the road, and Tori never changed into clean clothes unless she was given the chance to shower. She would simply remove her clothes each day when the time came after dark and tuck them into the saddlebags on Eddie's bike. Experience had taught her that failing to do so would have harsh consequences if one of the guys had to remove them. Then, after the night was over, she could put them back on for the day's ride, relatively clean, or at least cleaner than the alternative.

Unexpectedly, a young woman poked her head into the room, disturbing her thoughts and causing Tori to give a startled jump. "I'm sorry," the honey blond exclaimed, "am I interrupting?"

Tori just stared at the girl, amazed she was being spoken to by an outsider. By this time, she had pretty well guessed Eli only came to see her because it was part of his job, and therefore he had to talk to her. Judging from her clothing, which matched Tori's, this girl was also a guest of the hospital and her interjection was, therefore, surprising.

"Hi," Tori responded calmly in a low voice, trying to appear normal while tossing the hair that had fallen in front of the left side of her face behind her. As soon as she did so; however, Tori could see the shocked look flutter across the girl's features as she noticed the scar.

Immediately, the young woman tried to recover, but her smile was too large as she sputtered, "well, nice to meet you," gave a small half wave and quickly retreated down the hall.

Tori sat stunned for a moment on the edge of the bed, staring at the empty doorway. Finally, she slipped off her canvas shoes and moved to the head of the bed. Shoving her right shoulder into the corner as she squatted, she rested her forehead against the wall and drifted off to sleep.

Several hours later, she awoke to the sound of a gravelly voice and a firm hand shaking her left shoulder. Giving a sharp shout, she spun around slapping the hand away from her, sitting straight up with wide eyes and quickened breath. After a few moments of deep breathing, Tori realized she was looking into the face of an older black woman, with short grey hair and a gold tooth. While she stared at the tooth, she heard the voice say, "Youse gonna miss dinna now young'un," and then the woman turned and left the room.

Slowly, Tori stood up from the bed and pushed her feet back into the canvas slippers. Moving cautiously to the door, she looked down the hall, and noticed a couple of people moving down the passage in the direction they had entered from earlier that day. While considering whether she was actually hungry, her stomach gave a loud rumble, so she followed in the direction the others had taken in hopes of finding the cafeteria.

It only took a few minutes to locate the large room, off in the hallway to the left of the massive fountain. Inside, there was a flurry of chatter, as groups of people sat around circular tables, enjoying their dinner. Tori stepped into the room, and she could hear the drop in the noise level as several of the speaker's voices suddenly halted or dropped to a whisper.

Ignoring the stares, Tori made her way over to the stack of trays that marked the beginning of the cafeteria line. Taking one, she shuffled down, sliding the tray and selecting items for her meal. About halfway down the line, she became aware that the two women on the other side of the glass were standing, gaping at her.

At that moment, Tori would have headed back to her room had it not been for the relentless complaints of her intestines. With great purpose, she chose to move the tray along the metal bars, continuing to gather items. At the end, she stopped to look eye to eye with one of the women who served the drinks. "Water, please," she requested her voice barely above a whisper.

The drink was poured without a sound and the glass placed on her tray. Tori looked up at the woman's face. As soon as their eyes met, the woman shot her a quick, tense smile, then quickly dropped her gaze and turned away. With a heavy heart, she lifted her tray and headed for the tables.

It was a long walk to the far end of the room. Tori chose an empty table and sat her tray down upon it. Once she had, she realized now the real conundrum was at hand—exactly where to sit. In the past, it would not have mattered. When she was with the Dragons, she would have been safe and accepted no matter which seat she was sitting in. In this place, things were by no means as certain.

Should she sit with her back to the room, where she could eat in semi-privacy? Doing so meant the risk of having someone approach unseen from behind. And yet, the thought of sitting on the opposite side of the table, facing the room that was full of strangers staring in her direction was not any more appealing.

After a full minute of consideration, she compromised and sat halfway around the table, so that her back was to a wall, and the majority of the room was to her left and could be monitored using her peripheral vision. Straight in front of her, Tori could see the serving line and a handful of people exiting it. Curiously, all of those coming off the line and heading into the seating area were quickly waved over to an empty spot elsewhere in the dining room, and so the five other chairs at her table remained unfilled.

Step by Step

Tori was sitting in one of the padded chairs, knees curled to her chest and arms wrapped, when Eli Founder arrived the next morning. She had been sitting for some time, watching the sunrise bring light to the lush green outside her small window.

The Dragons slept and lived outdoors routinely, and she was beginning to feel penned up being indoors for so many days now. "How was the bed?" Eli asked as he took the seat opposite of her. A blank stare was her only response, so he mumbled a simple "Well, you'll get there," and let the subject drop.

Tori lay her left cheek on her knees, watching out into the patio for several minutes. Finally, in a low voice, she inquired, "Why am I here?"

Eli shifted in his seat, wanting to be precise with his words. "You're here for evaluation, and to heal." He drew a deep breath to continue, catching himself before he spoke, and then exhaled slowly in silence.

Tori's head popped up, and she asked again in a more forceful tone, "No, I mean why am I *here*." She added emphasis to the word 'here' by reaching out with her right hand to stab the table with her index finger.

At his surprised look, she continued with the irritation clear in her voice, "I told you the knife was mine. I told you the Dragons got what they deserved. I did it. I killed them. Why am I not in prison or a cell or something?" Tori uncurled her legs and began to move her hands around as she spoke. She was clearly distressed about her situation.

Eli drew another deep breath as he watched, again releasing it slowly. "This is very complicated," he spoke in his low, soothing tone. "I understand you feel very guilty right now, maybe wanting to be punished for your actions, but there are a lot of questions that must be answered before any judgments can be made."

Eli paused as Tori tilted her head in an odd fashion, giving him an angry look and almost growling, "What kind of questions?"

Thinking back to the meeting and the plan, he decided to simply lay it all out. "Well, for starters, we don't really know who you are, do we?" The question was flatter, like a statement, and he didn't pause for a reply. "Your ID was fake, and your identity has been completely untraceable up to this point."

Tori's jaw dropped in disbelief. She had never really considered who she was or where she had come from, *like it would matter*. She only knew she was Tori, the girl of the group, a Dragon as long as she could remember.

"So am I a prisoner here?" she demanded. "If not, I could just leave. I am 24 years old; I could just leave and go and do whatever I wanted to do." She was stammering a bit, not at all sure how her words would be taken or if a punishment would come raining down. But, Eli just barked a short laugh of amusement and shook his head.

"You're not 24, Tori. Your ID was fake. The whole thing was fake. The only thing on it that is accurate is the picture; it looks like you. By the doctor's best estimate, you are not even 15 yet," he took great care to stick to the details he had been given.

Tori stared at him, mouth still slightly open, in a state of shock, and he shifted in his seat under her stern gaze. He continued slowly, trying to be more wary of her feelings, *flies and honey and all that*, "Look, we had a meeting, a committee of people, after you were found. Together, we decided how to handle your situation, because quite frankly, it's pretty unique. What we need to do first, is find out who you are, and we have a team working on that. Second, we need to find out everything we can about you—where have you been, what you have experienced, are you educated? We are going to need you to cooperate and tell us everything you can about your life. Anything and everything you can remember."

Pausing, he leaned back in his chair, feeling the need to reach out to her. "It's going to be hard for you. We know you have been through a lot, and we want to help you, if you will let us."

Tori sat glaring at the man across the table, her mind racing, searching through memories, trying to find something that would debunk everything he had just said. She couldn't find it. All she could remember was Eddie and Red and the rest of the Dragons. And Henry. Henry, who had been there for her all those years. When she spoke, her voice was barely audible. "Why didn't you just let me die?"

Eli eyed her carefully, giving a long pause before responding. "That's not what we do, Tori. We don't kill people, and we don't 'just let them die.' We save them and help them. That's what we are going to do for you, if you will allow us to." She could see the lump in his throat move as he swallowed. "For now, we have an appointment to keep." To punctuate his statement, he rose and waited for her to join him at the door.

While Eli led her through the halls of the facility, he began to notice a pattern in the reactions of the people as they spotted her. He had come to think of her as a beautiful person, but he was fairly certain that was not the cause of the double takes and stares she was now receiving.

Thinking about the committee, he hoped Debra Paisley, who was in charge of integrating Tori into society after this was over, would find what could be done to remove or cover the scar that marred the girl's pretty face. This short walk had made him very aware of what a huge block this small thing had the potential to be for her.

Arriving at the entrance to Dr. Lawrence Carlisle's office, Eli took a step inside to shake his hand and introduce Tori before heading out. Then, giving her a quick pat on the shoulder and encouraging smile, he bade softly, "Good luck! I will see you in a few days."

"A few days?" Tori echoed, taken by surprise. As much as she disliked his visits, she disliked the thought of not having them even more.

"Sure—other business. You'll be fine." Not wanting to drag things out, he walked away with a quick wave of his hand in goodbye.

Tori stared after him for a moment, and then took a slow look around the room from the doorway before sitting in one of the large, leather covered chairs on the patient side of the desk. The office seemed crowded by the size of the furniture, all dark stained wood and burgundy colored leather.

There were two large floor-to-ceiling bookcases on either side of the door, and a full wall made of glass on the left hand side behind the desk that looked out into the sun covered foliage outside. Dr. Carlisle himself was a middle aged man with a balding head and wire framed glasses. There were pictures of his family scattered around the room, all smiling at her.

Overwhelmed by the feeling she had missed out on far more than she had realized, she folded her hands in her lap and stared across the desk at the doctor, who studied her for a few moments before he began speaking. "That's some scar," he finally began. "Mind telling me how you got it?"'

Tori's nostrils flared as she took a deep breath. She did mind telling him about it and considered saying so. "Eddie Farrell gave it to me so that people wouldn't talk to me," she finally stated flatly.

The doctor continued to study her for a moment, then leaned forward in his chair to place his forearms on his desk. "I see," he replied "and do you always answer questions in fifteen words or less? I mean that could have made a nice story and told me a great deal about you."

Perfectly calm, Tori met his gaze, but chose to ignore the question. After several more minutes of silence, the doctor reached for his pen and made a few notes on the yellow notepad next to him. Then, standing, he gave her a half smile and commanded, "Let's go for a walk."

After leaving the office, the doctor led Tori out through a glass door and into the garden that made up the heart of the building. As they walked along the winding path, he decided to take a different approach. "You know we are going to try to help you, right?"

Again in a flat tone, "yes, I know," was her response.

"Very well then," continued the doctor. "So we are going to need to set some ground rules here I think. I can see you are accustomed to only giving exactly what you have been asked to share and no more. In some instances that can be a good thing, but here, what you need to do most is talk. You need to share everything, and I do mean everything, including the things that cause you pain, fear or sadness, as well as the things that make you happy. Do you understand?"

Stopping abruptly, Tori looked irritated, her eyes shifting around rapidly as if she were searching for something that had just slipped out of sight. Finally, she looked straight at him and replied, "Dr. Carlisle, I only ever feel one thing, and that's anger. You can't hurt me. I don't feel happy; I don't feel sad. Everyone I have ever known or cared about is dead. I have spent my whole life in the midst of a group of street thugs and criminals who did terrible things to me and made me do terrible things to other people. I killed those men. I don't really know what you or anyone else wants from me. The only thing I do know is that Henry told me one day I would have a different life, and now I think that maybe, somehow, this is how I am going to get it. That is the only reason I am standing here, talking to you right now. Because I promised that I would."

The frankness of her words brought a smile to the doctor's thin lips. "Well, there you go. That is a start. Of course, this isn't going to be easy for you, and you may find that you feel or care about more than you realized or wanted to. For right now, we need to come up with a plan for what you are going to do to get better or improve your life as it were. First off..." and the doctor laid out his plan for meetings and journals, testing and educational experiences he felt were needed to help her get in touch with her inner self and begin to prepare for the rest of her life.

Tori just stared at him. She could feel the anger boiling inside of her, and for a moment she was severely tempted to knock him to the ground and punch him a few times. Resisting the urge, she simply stood there listening and hoping for the strength to make it through what was to come.

After he finished outlining what her schedule was going to look like, the doctor led her to the cafeteria where she was allowed to eat. Leaving her to her meal, Tori made her way through the line alone just as she had before. Carrying her tray with deliberate steps, she returned to the same corner chair that she had deemed the most functional. She ate in a wary state, always monitoring the comings and goings of others, her mind turning over the conversations of Eli and Dr. Carlisle. The two seemed to align perfectly, and she allowed herself to consider the possibility they were genuinely intending to help her.

After lunch, Tori began taking tests to evaluate her education. She had been reluctant to share that she had never actually seen the inside of a classroom. Fortunately for her, it was decided that it would be easier to simply run a battery of exams and see where her strengths and weaknesses lay.

Dr. Carlisle explained that he had already contacted one of the local colleges in search of any students who would be willing to tutor her in subjects she was lacking, but Tori wasn't real fond of the idea. As she sat staring at the page of questions that first day, she couldn't help wondering if she should give it her best, or just randomly mark answers and be done with it.

In the end, it was her pride and Henry's memory that won out. Besides, if they were going to make her learn the parts she didn't know, it was pointless to do poorly on purpose and then suffer being tutored because of it. Making her choice, she went to great lengths to work through each problem the best she could.

After a few hours of working, Tori was set free to explore the hospital on her own, which she rather preferred to being around people. First, she made her way through the garden, taking in the sounds and smells. Along one of the paths, she found a stone bench, where she camped out for almost an hour watching birds busily visiting flowers and flitting around. She sat, enjoying the warm late afternoon sun on her upturned face while the musical chirps and whistles echoed around her.

Tori recognized a few of the species and her mind began to drift back through the years, back before everything got ugly with the Dragons, back to the time when they were her teachers and mentors. In fact, even though Henry was her dearest friend, it was only a small part of what she knew that had come from him.

Marcus Sanchez had been the one to teach her about birds. He knew all about them—species, habitats, and behaviors. He was also the one who gave her the best Spanish lessons and would tell her stories he had heard as a boy; stories that made her laugh or cry, back before she forgot what it was like to feel and show emotion. As Tori sat remembering, a pang of sadness touched her, and she thought about the small camp they had occupied "in the bush" of South America as the Dragons called it.

It wasn't much, a small clearing where a rough cabin that formed the kitchen and chow hall stood, surrounded by light jungle that served as the sleeping quarters in small tents or hammocks and lean-tos. Even the ground under one of the metal patios or awnings would do for a nap. It was often hot there, and when the rains came, it seemed to last for days and weeks at a time. In a way, it was the only home she had ever known; out in the open where the wind, sun and rain were better than walls and windows, and the Dragons were her family.

Shaking off the past, Tori stood, stretched, and headed inside to explore the rest of the building while she had the chance. Heading on around what turned out to be a large square building that made a complete loop, with a garden area in the middle, she discovered two other things that made the hospital almost likable.

The first was the library. Tori had always had a love for books and the places they could take her. In their old cabin, the Dragons had built a bookcase for her books that covered an entire wall. When they hit the road, she had only been allowed to keep one book in her pack at a time. Now, there was a whole room full of them, a sight that made her heart thump with anticipation.

The second discovery was even better—she found the gym. Inside there was a treadmill, weights, an overhead bar, and ropes for climbing and jumping. The Dragons had always kept themselves fit, and had taught her how to train and exercise regularly, even when there wasn't a lot of fancy equipment around to use. Tori had not bothered trying to work out since the farmhouse, but now realized she had missed the physical activity and would relish being able to train again.

Making her way back to her room, she mentally worked out a schedule for herself. She had checked out a book from the Library, "A History of Ancient Egypt," and could not wait to delve into the pages. When she arrived back in her small quarters, she set the clock on the dresser for 5 am, just to be sure she was awake early enough to hit the gym before breakfast.

Finally, heading to the cafeteria for dinner, she took the book with her to read while she ate.

Now it wouldn't matter that her table was empty, and no one spoke to her. She had the world at her fingertips and no one to bother her, and that was just the way she wanted it.

Keeping Fit

Now that she had physical exercise, Tori did not feel like such an outsider in her new home. She woke up by 5 am every morning and headed to the gym. It was early, so she seldom had to share it with anyone else. The room was small, only about 25 foot by 25 foot, so the amount of equipment was kept low, with only one of most everything.

As she stepped inside, a mirror that covered floor to ceiling ran down the wall that was immediately on her right. Tori hated mirrors. She would rather not see the scars of her life staring back at her, so she would keep her head down or her back to it as much as possible.

To the left of the door stood the treadmill, and next to it a stair-climber. She would have rather run in the garden, but it was clearly not designed for such activity, so the treadmill would have to do. Between them and the left corner lay a 2 inch thick foam mat and a set of hooks positioned on the wall with four jumping ropes of different lengths hanging from them. She had become quite skilled with the jumping rope, doing double and triple-unders with ease. She shuddered, recalling some of the more gruesome skills she had learned for short pieces of rope.

Half way between the two corners of the wall, a climbing rope hung from the extra tall ceiling. Tori felt a jolt of excitement as she looked up to see the ceiling extended a full two stories; allowing for more strenuous climbs. She used to push herself at climbing when she was young, always wanting to be faster than the time before, and would enjoy the challenge here.

Still gazing upwards, she noticed the two fans that ran to efficiently cool the air below during her workouts, positioned on the opposite end of the ceiling as the climbing rope. Looking up at them now, their breeze on her face made her feel like she was back in the bush, the warm moist air pushing in on her from all sides.

Along the far wall, in the opposite corner of the padded mat, there stood a small lifting area. There were only a few free weights with a single bar, but it could be set up to 300 pounds, which was more than enough. There was no bench, but Tori had never gotten used to using one anyways.

In the center of the far wall stood a large metal shelving unit that held a nice variety of kettlebells and medicine ball weights, along with three different sized boxes for jumping. Memories of how to train using those pieces came flooding back to her, almost bringing a smile to her lips. Almost.

Tori felt most pleased with the overhead bar and the set of rings that stood straight in front of the door. They faced the door and out into the room so that she could avoid the mirror, and she could do a variety of leg lifting routines, as well as dip, pull up, and hanging exercises. The space was small, but well thought out, and she quickly realized how grateful she was to have this place to call her own.

As she worked, she recalled her first training days and how hard Brian Turner had pushed her as she grew up in the wild of South America. He had been in charge of her physical training, and he took that job very seriously.

Brian would wake her every morning at first light for a run, which was Tori's least favorite part. They would follow paths through the tall trees, winding around their small camp like a maze. She learned to keep her footing, even when the ground was rocky or slick.

In time, she grew strong and bound easily over the patches of uneven ground that rose and fell, allowing her small and agile frame to scoot quickly up the slope and slide down the other side with ease. By the time they hit the road, she beat her mentor around the loop regularly and was proud of her speed and strength. She almost felt wistful as the memories danced around her.

After the run, it would be sit-ups, squats and

lunges. He changed their routine often to keep it fresh, and the movements became second nature to her. She never became bulky or overly muscular, but rather strong over all of her muscle groups.

He taught her about pull ups and push-ups, which strengthened her shoulders and chest. This allowed her to easily climb the trees that hid their small camp, and she gained a certain zeal for doing so. Many a hot afternoon, she would climb into a tall tree and look down and out at the world around her.

Her favorite, a Tabebuia Impetiginosa, or pink trumpet tree, which would sprout bright pink flowers that glittered about her, stood at the edge of the territory the Dragons called their own. She would climb that tree staring out across the tops of the trees that grew down the slopes below it, and wonder about the world outside of their jungle home.

Brian had made her do hundreds upon hundreds of leg raises, bringing her toes to the bar from which she hung, giving her a strong stomach and core. They seldom used weights, except for a small range of kettlebells and medicine balls that made the exercise more difficult. Tori often felt exhausted afterwards, as Brian never seemed to have a set plan and would go on endlessly. He simply pushed her until she was exhausted, then pushed her some more.

Thinking back now, Tori was grateful for what Brian had given her, and used those old familiar exercises to regain her strength and feel relaxed in this strange place. She knew now he had been training her for a terrible purpose, but vowed to herself that one day she would make it right.

After about an hour of physical fitness in the tiny gym, Tori would scramble back to her room for a shower before breakfast. The time beneath the waves of warm water soothed her spirit, and she cherished it deeply. She only wished the water could remove the stains she could see on her hands through her mind's eye. She could scrub them, but the blemishes were always present, even though no one else could see them. Standing in the shower, she would will herself not to see the marks, and sometimes she was able to make them fade. Most of the time, they remained, a crimson blotch that caused her heart to ache. This was something she was loathe to share with anyone, especially the good doctor and his endlessly prying ways.

As a side effect of the testing, Tori became concerned about her education. Having never attended school, she really did not know how much she had missed out on, and did not want to be left behind. However, after evaluating her scores, Dr. Carlisle seemed very pleased with her range of knowledge and told her higher education might be in her future, but for now she was in a good place, whatever that meant. So, she was content to continue to educate herself as she had always done, checking out books from the library that would give her new knowledge about the world.

Tori always took her book with her to the cafeteria, sitting alone reading while she ate. The other patients in the facility had become accustomed to her presence, so the stares had all but died away. She had even met several in group sessions, but they did not go out of their way to speak to her, and she felt no need to push the issue.

Instead, she would go through the line, choosing her fruits, vegetables and meats, then head to her corner table, always taking the same chair so that the room was to her left, and she could be ready should anyone ever approach her. No one ever did.

Henry had taught Tori to never stop learning, never stop growing. He was the Dragon, who had given her a taste for philosophy and history and a love of art and music. He had encouraged her to wonder why things are the way they are. He sparked in her a desire to always be more than she was, and she felt that she was honoring his memory by pushing herself to follow what meant the most to him. Tori had learned to speak every language he spoke, and would spend hours listening to his stories. He never grew tired of her endless questions, and seemed to enjoy imparting his wisdom to her.

As a precaution in this new place, Tori had

purposely not mentioned to anyone that she spoke and read French, German, Spanish and Russian, as well as she did English. The Dragons used a variety of languages to keep their affairs private in the company of outsiders, and she had learned them all before she was even old enough to know there was a difference.

Now that the Dragons were gone, she kept the knowledge hidden. She knew most people only spoke one language, or maybe two, and realized it was to her advantage not to reveal everything about herself if she could avoid it.

However, about a week after her arrival, Eli surprised her with a collection of fairy tales written in German. She had suffered a visit from Warren La Buff the day before, which had sent her into an angry tirade. The man purposely goaded her into a fight, and she ended up losing her temper during the meeting. She had sprayed him with a plethora of German insults and curses as he departed, then later regretted giving up that piece of herself.

At the time, Eli presented his gift; she had

remained stone faced at the offering, but inside she was ecstatic, first because of the book itself, and second because it had come from him. No one would ever take Henry's place, but Eli was carving out his own spot in her heart, bit by bit. In a shy voice, she managed to suppress her grin as she admitted that she could, in fact, read the small tome, and offered a small thank you through the forced calm she projected.

After that, Tori was given a set of language tests, and she reluctantly demonstrated her skills as a polyglot. Eli seemed thrilled, and adopted French as their private language, since he was fluent in it, as well. This brought her a small amount of recompense as she loved sharing something private with her new friend, and they used the language often thereafter.

Tori's afternoons were spent in a variety of therapy sessions. During private meetings with Dr. Carlisle, he would probe her with questions about her life. At first, she was very averse to sharing any details with him, not wanting to talk about all the things that had happened to her—things she wanted to forget rather than face, like fear and shame.

Right away, he stumbled upon the name Henry and noticed she had a fondness for this man. Grasping it like a desperate straw, he kept returning to her most tender topic until she caved and began to share more about the man who had been most like a father to her.

Henry Morgan was not an exceedingly tall man, only standing a tad over six foot, and a lean 220 pounds. He was muscular in build and kept himself fit for his age, often joining Brian and Tori in their morning regimen. He never interfered in Brian's directives, as that was Brian's role to play, but he seemed to enjoy watching as their young charge learned and grew strong in her physical fitness routines.

He had sandy brown hair, at least the parts of it that had not gone grey were, and dark brown eyes. His complexion was a deep tan from years in the sun, which had caused the delicate skin around his eyes to grow thin and wrinkled too soon. He also had a warm smile that always made her feel that she was cared for, even in the darkest times she would face, for as long as he was alive.

As she described him to the doctor, Tori felt a heavy ache deep inside her chest. Henry had a strong voice, which he kept low when he spoke to her. His hands were large and leathery, but soft when he placed them on her. She would never have said that she loved this man; he was her friend and her mentor. However, even she had to admit, he had stirred feelings within her no other man ever had, and she doubted ever would again.

Raising a Dragon

Tori had been with the Dragons for many years; longer than she could remember. They had educated her when she was young, giving her the basics and knowledge she would need to function as a member of their team. During that time, Henry and three others were her caretakers and teachers. They remained at the camp with her full time, while the rest of the group came and went with the seasons. Eddie was the leader of that portion of their small society, and Tori had to admit, she was not disappointed each time they rolled out of the camp, leaving her to her favorites.

As her primary guardian, Henry had been responsible for Tori's daily needs. He saw to it that she ate, bathed, and had clean clothes to wear. Because of this, she felt safe in his arms, and would often sneak out of her bed to curl up next to him during the night. A few times, she went so far as to call him her 'real daddy,' which he emphatically denied and warned her not to say in front of any of the others.

Most of the time, he would send her back to her own hammock, but sometimes he would hold her in his arms and allow her to sleep there. The feel of his breath rising and falling comforted her as he blew warm air across the side of her head and the top of her ear, and she cherished the memory fondly for ever after.

While sharing Henry's hammock, Tori would sleep with her back to his chest, and he would often drape his arm around her, his hand rubbing her stomach through the cloth or his thumb gently lifting her shirt to rub a small circle around her belly button to give a small tickle. She felt completely safe and accepted in that place.

It was a feeling that never carried over to any of the others, and she never cared to be that close to any of them, especially the man who claimed to be her father. As she grew older, she became aware that the group of men were playing kind of tug of war, only Tori was the rope, being pulled in all directions as each man in the camp, especially Henry and Eddie, wanted to garner the lion's share of her time and affection.

Each time the traveling portion of their group returned to the camp, Eddie grew more impatient and demanding of her time. He was evidently disappointed that she had grown taller, but still had not undergone any other changes. He intended to wait until she looked like a woman, and her body matched her age, before they promoted her to her next role within the group. Only then would they finalize her training and take her out of the camp.

The group was anxious because her maturity was so late in coming; late enough to become a cause for real concern. At one point, a heated discussion had taken place as to what should be done if it did not begin soon. With a fair amount of convincing and no alternative, it was reluctantly agreed they would leave her in Henry's charge one last time.

Eddie was outwardly angry and disgusted things weren't going as smoothly as he had planned, and in a fit of drunken rage beat her soundly before leaving her that last time. This fact only made her all the more happy to see them roll out before the rainy season started, and to secretly hope he would never return.

Sadly, Eddie did return to the camp, and he seemed quite relieved, as did they all, to find she had finally begun to grow curves. Their bikes were stored for the last time, and the traveling group would remain in the camp until she was ready to leave with them after a couple of years of polishing. Tori's final training commenced, and her lessons bore down heavily upon her as Eddie taught her tactics for fighting and to use a variety of weapons.

The camp now full of the men she mostly chose to avoid, and her training beginning to include things she did not understand or want to learn, Tori wanted to share the hammock with Henry more and more. She craved his company and the peace it gave her to be close to him, which he tried to deny her. Giving him her best wide-eyed gazes, her soft blue orbs enticed him to relent, and eventually his hammock became theirs.

For some time, she slept there to avoid the others, but eventually she began to have strange feelings and thoughts that made her question her own motives. Tori could feel her body changing, and loved the excited flutter that it gave her when Henry would lay his arm across her belly as he always had.

Now when Henry would stroke the line of her front, it caused her breath to quicken and become ragged. She had discovered two knots that had formed in her chest before the group had reunited, and now they had grown into large mounds that required larger garments to hide. At the same time, a thin mat of hair sprang up to cover her delicate female folds of flesh.

Tori was becoming a woman, and her rush of hormones brought new challenges for her to face. She was completely disgusted to discover exactly what being a woman entailed, and mortified that she had to ask Henry for help with the issue. He took the news calmly and provided her with a book that explained all the details she needed to know. She was relieved that none of the others mentioned the occurrences, although she was certain they were aware of her condition.

Of course, it was no wonder they had noticed the changes that had been taking place. Her swollen chest had forced her to take to wearing some of the men's shirts to cover herself fully. They allowed her to do so as they seemed to enjoy her new look, albeit from a distance more or less. Of course, as everyone became accustomed to her shapeliness, things brewed below the surface, and everyone could tell their days in the camp were coming to an end.

Tori had begun to feel uncomfortable with the way the rest of the group watched her. Several times, she sensed she was being spied upon when she moved about the camp, especially when she bathed. She also became aware that the other men seemed to be looking for occasions to touch her, or press their bodies against her. This caused her a great deal of distress, and she found new and unwanted advances almost frightening. She longed for things to be as they had always been, and yet she was just as affected by the changes as the rest of the group.

At the time, Tori was not aware that Eddie had forbidden any of the group to touch her, and Henry had no intention of going against the command. However, her lying with him in the darkness was taking its toll on them, as she was becoming anxiously aware of his hardened state as it pressed against her while he slept. The situation caused new and strange thoughts to rage inside her confused mind, and she loved the idea of his touching her, longing for him to explore her forbidden places.

The nights and days ran together for her, filled with yearning she could not understand and Henry refused to acknowledge. She felt tormented by his unwillingness to do anything more than provide her with books that explained the process of what was happening to her, and although she poured over them endlessly, they left her with more questions than they answered.

In the light of day, Tori knew she had to be patient, but in the cover of darkness, she began to toy with him, pressing her body against his until he relented and began to explore her more fully. He began by caressing her through her thin cotton tees and shorts, but refused to move into the realm of bare skin. Even this small amount of attention had her panting, and she yielded easily to his touch, frustrated that the act only left her wanting more.

In the weeks and months they shared in this manner; Tori's needs became stronger. Henry's stroking had begun to make her moist between her legs during the night. In the morning, she would have a thick mass of clear mucus wetting her panties, and she would do her best to hide what plagued her thoughts the most. Her need was becoming raw within her, and she was growing afraid that the others might see it and know her unclean thoughts.

In desperation, she began to seek out locations where she could clean herself and explore her hidden areas in private. She allowed herself to wonder about Henry, to think and dream about his body. She yearned to run her hands across his chest that was covered in a thick carpet of dark curls, and hated the way he kept it hidden from her now, seldom removing his shirt when she was close enough to steal a caress.

Inside her head, Tori felt as if she were going mad, unable to stop the random feelings of desire. Her mind was no longer easy to control, and her thoughts were often distracted to a singular idea—the craving to be touched in the darkness by the one man who seemed completely unwilling to do so.

Just when she felt she couldn't take anymore, Eddie announced her training had come to an end, and it would soon be time to leave the camp for good. In celebration of the event, Paul Edwards and David Long were sent to the nearest metropolis to shop for her new wardrobe and their final load of supplies.

Tori had never left the camp before and could only imagine the world around her through her books and the stories that the men shared with her. Knowing she was getting new clothes thrilled her, and scared her at the same time, as things were changing so quickly now around her, and it was completely beyond her control.

When the pair returned to the camp, they presented her with two pairs of new jeans, shirts in her new size, several pairs of lacy panties, and two new bras to hold her swollen badges of womanhood. She had never seen or owned a bra before, and explored them for several minutes, pulling on the elastic straps and fingering the tiny hooks. She could feel her face flush as she realized what they were for.

The twelve men that made up the Dragons had gathered around as she was presented with her new wardrobe, and she now felt shy standing before them. Tori had spent her whole life in this place with these men, but things were shifting now, and a feeling of anxiety twinged in the back of her mind. She smiled nervously as she looked around the circle of familiar faces, but the eyes that stared back at her were changed, darker now, the smiles more like snarls dripping with lust.

There was a scent in the air she had never

smelt before, and it struck fear deep inside her. Tori said her thank-yous to her two benefactors, and as the darkness fell made her way to the small cabin to make dinner as usual. Still, she could not help but think about the evening's events, and the sense that something terrible was moving towards her.

Later that night, after the meat and potatoes were gone, the group disbanded to their usual places of rest. Henry helped Tori put out the fire and clean up the cabin that served as their kitchen in silence. She could feel him watching her, as he had done many times before, but this night she found no comfort in his gaze. She was suddenly overcome with fear; fear that she might get her wish and finally feel his hands upon her bare flesh.

When the last of the chores were finished, Tori looked around the small room, desperately searching for some other task to occupy her for a few more minutes. As her eyes roamed, Henry sidled up beside her, placing his hands on her hip and waist, pushing them around to embrace and pull her in front of him. She had reached an equal height to him long ago, and he found her mouth easily as he leaned forward slightly to kiss her.

Tori allowed the kiss, but her body stiffened and she could hear her heart pounding in her ears. She had wanted this, but now that the moment was at hand, she felt petrified with the realization of it. His lips moved over hers; he nuzzled her cheek, sliding his hand up her back to the nape of her neck. His fingers massaged the tender areas of her neckline and scalp, and his other hand made a circle over the small of her back, and she could feel his hardness pressed against the front of her.

Tori grew even tenser, panic rising inside of her, but Henry was patient, stepping back and grasping her hand. With his free hand, he dowsed the light of the cabin and led her out into the darkness, across the camp to their hammock. There was no sign of the others, but Tori could not overcome the sensation of being watched.

When they reached the hammock, Henry stopped, dropping her hand while turning to face her. Grasping the hem of his shirt, he lifted it over his head and let it fall to the ground. Standing before him, Tori could see the light of a full moon sifting through the shadows of the trees above them, and falling on the mass of hairs that covered his chest, glistening silver and black. She swallowed hard as she stared at the rise and fall of the thick rug as he breathed, calmly waiting for her to respond.

Nervously, she moved to survey their surroundings, but he quickly caught her waist, pulling her to him again, with a warning to keep her eyes and mind on him. "There is nothing out there for you now, baby girl," he whispered against the curve of her neck, "lay with me." He seemed nervous, and she wondered briefly why he had finally given in to her open advances of the last few months.

As he held her, their bodies swaying gently in the breeze, Tori raised her right hand and allowed her fingers to slide through the thick curls covering his chest. She could feel his breath heaving beneath her fingers as she found a nipple and twirled her finger around it. She lowered her face to peek at it, her breath tickled him and causing him to shudder.

Instantly, Tori became lost in a rush of emotion, as the weeks and months of impure thoughts caught up to her. She worked her fingers more deeply into his pelt, feeling the hardness of the muscle below. Her left hand moved around to his smooth, moist back, pressing him tighter against her.

Turning her face upward, she moved to kiss him, and he pressed his mouth against hers. She had never kissed a man before, and found the experience thrilling as she tasted him and felt the brush of his short whiskers against her soft skin. He was not gentle in his actions, and Tori became enflamed with his urgency.

Stepping back a short way, she grabbed her own shirt and peeled it away just as he had done. Going a step further, she stripped away the rest of her clothing just as quickly, relishing the cool air that soothed her burning skin and enjoying the full rush of her desire to feel his hands upon her. Henry did not make her wait.

As they closed the short distance between them, he started at her hips, sliding his fingers easily up along her waist to cup her breasts, allowing his thumbs to slide gently across her firm points. Their hands became frantic as they slid over one another's bodies, Tori uttering a small groan of annoyance at meeting the top of his pants on the way down to explore him further.

With a free hand, Henry pulled the button and zipper of his jeans loose, allowing them to fall in one motion. He took a step back out of the leggings and boots, and then tightened his arm, moving her with him towards the hammock. Leaning back into the swing, he stretched out, and she quickly scrambled on top of him, sliding slightly to one side so that she could continue to explore his nakedness.

She found his manhood stiff and swollen, her fingers trembling as she moved from the tip to the base, eager to uncover all the secrets it might possess. Henry's hand moved to her face, and he traced the line of her jaw with his fingertips, sliding them to her lips to part them and sneak his thumb inside. As he retracted the thumb, she turned slightly, folding herself so that she could reach him and slip her tongue around the head of his shaft before taking him into her mouth and massaging him for several minutes.

While Tori busily pleasured her lover, he explored the parts of her he had never explored. His fingers slid down along her back; he reached the top of her buttocks and delved into the crack between. As he pushed his fingers down, they raked across the folding skin of her rear, and she startled slightly at the unfamiliar touch.

Not stopping, Henry pushed further down and around until he reached the moist folds of skin and hair that covered her small opening, then slipped his fingers inside the hot wet hollow. As he pushed his fingers deeper, he was able to reach the hard pebble that hid beneath its small coat of flesh, and massaged it with a free finger as her tongue made slow laps around the head of him, teasing him as she worked.

Finally, he had to stop her before she finished him, as he wanted to save that until he had found his way inside her. Tori lifted her head and looked at him with questioning eyes, and his lips curved into a smile as he sucked on the fingers that were now covered in her gooey glaze.

With a pulling motion, he turned her so that she was beneath him in the hammock, her legs spread as he kneeled between her knees. He looked down at her, their bodies bathed in moonlight, and he stared into her eyes as he pushed himself forward until he was inside of her. Tori was not prepared for the sharp pain the motion brought, and the air was forced from her lungs in a spasm of agony as he fully took her and rested on top of her.

Lying still and allowing her to catch her breath, he continued to gaze into her deep pools of blue moon glow. Tori clawed at his chest and back for a moment, small gasps of pain escaping her wide open mouth. Henry's eyes dropped to her moist swollen lips, then returned to her sensual eyes, as he moved his right hand up to push through her long tresses and rest against the side of her head in a comforting fashion.

Sliding his thumb over the skin on her face in front of her ear, he lowered his mouth to hers, gently kissing her lips and nuzzling her cheek.

Soon, the pain subsided, and she began to respond to his caresses, able to breathe more normally. When he began to flex his hips, moving inside of her, tears slipped from her eye and dropped onto the hand that covered her ear as it soothed her.

A Walk in the Park

Tori sat in the chair, nervously rubbing her finger across the metal beads that ran along the arms. She had no idea what had possessed her to share her story about Henry, and now that she had, she was ashamed of what they had done. Although her face showed no emotion, a deep sadness gripped her, as she recalled it was the last time he had ever touched her.

Wanting her to continue, Dr. Carlisle sat patiently waiting, an encouraging smile teasing the corners of his lips, but she did not. With a small sigh, he allowed the story to end, but made a note to pick up there again later. "You're making fine progress," he said aloud as he stood and walked her to the door of his office. Tori made no reply. Instead, she stepped into the hall and headed towards the fountain.

When she reached the foyer of the building, she sat on the stone edge of the giant spout that had taken her breath away the day she arrived. Her mind was still lost, trapped in the bush country of Brazil. Staring at the water and then closing her eyes, Tori listened to the murmur of the running water, her skin warmed by the rays of the sun that shown in through the glass above her. She wasn't sure how long she had been sitting there, when a familiar and friendly voice called her name.

Tori raised her head to find Special Agent Eli Founder standing next to her, grinning from ear to ear, as usual. Tori considered this for a moment, finding it confusing that he would always be in such good spirits when he visited her, and suspected he was actually high.

Reluctantly, she rose and they walked together towards the cafeteria in silence. Eli was becoming quite accustomed to her temperamental behavior, so her actions did little to surprise him. Earlier that day, he had a crazy thought occur to him, and he was especially excited at the possibilities. Yet, now that he was with her, he felt nervous at the prospect of having to propose the idea to Tori, and eventually to the Committee. Eli wanted Tori to come and live with him when she was released from the hospital, in his spare room.

He knew it wasn't part of the plan, but he had been thinking that she would need a place. If she did not go to prison, since she had no family to go to if none could be found, it would be a place she would be accepted. As they walked on without speaking, he got cold feet and suddenly thought better of mentioning it now, opting for a better time to make a suggestion.

After collecting their trays, the pair made their way to Tori's usual spot and began eating. Her somber mood continued, and Eli began to grow uncomfortable, realizing this was more than her typical behavior. When they had finished their meal, she had still not spoken a word to him, so after they dropped off their dirty trays, he guided her out into the garden, where they walked until they found her bench and sat down. Tori sat to his right and leaned her chin against her hands as her elbows dug into her knees in a slumping position.

Eli leaned back against the large tree that grew behind half of the bench like a chair back, reaching over with his right hand to run his fingers lightly down her spine. The action touched Tori much deeper than her skin, and she sat back slightly so that she could cock her head just a bit and peer at him over her left shoulder. Continuing to stroke her, he playfully pushed her hair out of the way and smiled at her, waiting her for to speak.

After several minutes of petting, Tori sat back, taking her half of the tree, "I told Dr. Carlisle something I shouldn't have."

Eli eyed her suspiciously for a moment before he asked, "What do you mean 'shouldn't have?' I think you are allowed to tell him anything you like."

"No," Tori continued, her face clearly drawn in pain, "not this. I told him about something that happened between Henry and I. Something private and special that should never have been told to anyone." She blinked quickly to stop the tears from falling, but it was too late, as Eli had already noticed them welling up in her crystal blue eyes.

She turned away from him and sat watching the birds as they danced lightly in the sunlight. Today, it did not cheer her, and she slumped forward again, elbows on her knees. When he raised his hand to stroke her, she turned her head to beg, "Please don't touch me," so he dropped his hand and waited. He had never seen her show any emotion other than anger and realized that even though this was painful for her, she was actually coming to a better place.

After an extended wait, he finally asked what he could do, so Tori leaned against the tree once more, briskly brushing away the tracks on her cheeks. Then, looking at him from the corner of her eye, asked in a low voice, "Would you like to hear my story?"

Immediately his heart began to pound. *The*

same story she just said she shouldn't have told?

His shock was evident on his face, so she went on to explain, "I told him the beginning, but I didn't even come close to finishing it. Besides, I think it would be better if you heard it." Tori stopped there, but in her heart she knew Eli was her special friend, and that someday she would have to share her past with him.

Eli pursed his lips as he considered the possible outcomes of letting her speak and the goal he had to reach. On the one hand, she had never been willing to divulge her past so readily, and he was now eager to hear what she had to say. On the other hand, the fact she had told the story once already and felt remorse at doing so, meant allowing it could backfire, and there would be a heavy price to pay in the end.

After weighing both sides equally, he gave his reply, "Tell me whatever you like, and I will keep your words in confidence." Immediately, Eli wished he had not felt the need to lie.

"We should go back inside then," she

responded with apprehension as she looked around the foliage that surrounded them. Although she seldom saw others along the paths, the chance of being overheard was too great to remain seated in the sunshine, even if they were speaking French.

Back inside her tiny room, Tori closed the door and then moved to sit on her bed with her back against the bathroom wall. Eli paused for a moment, then slipping off his shoes as she had done, curled up beside her, back to the wall, as well.

Tori reached over, grabbed her pillow and hugged it tightly to her chest. Inhaling deeply, she glanced at the man sitting beside her for a moment, and then looked down at her lap before she began to speak. Slowly, she retold the same story for Eli as closely as she could to what she recalled for Dr. Carlisle. However, she did not stop this time and finished out the nights event's for him in detail. After she had finished, she paused to take a peek at his reaction.

He was staring at her intently as she spoke,

and as her eyes shifted to meet his, he muttered, "Wow. That's really something. I really don't know what to say."

"You don't have to say anything," she stated in a low tone. "But if you are not ready to run out the door at this point, I might as well tell you the rest. Or more of the rest, I guess." Eli nodded his agreement to listen on, so Tori took another deep, cleansing breath, and then dove into the events that followed.

Into the Darkness

What had happened between Henry and Tori had not been private in the camp, as most of the other Dragons hid off in the shadow of the trees to watch. The next morning, unaware that Eddie was furious, Tori put on her old clothes, not wanting to wear the new ones.

She felt as if she were still naked whenever one of them looked her way. By lunch time, it was more than she could stand, so she headed through the trails to the north end of their land, until she found her favorite pink trumpet tree.

As she climbed, her heart raced, and she did not stop until she had reached the highest point she dared to climb into the thinning branches. Once she had chosen her perch, she sat on the swaying limb, allowing the breeze to splash across her face and upturned nose until the sun sank low in the sky.

Finally, she realized that there was no point in staying in the tree, as anyone who wanted her could simply climb up as well. As she began to descend, her stomach gave a low growl of hunger, but she muttered for it to shut up, as food was now the least of her worries.

The sun had almost set when she arrived back at the cabin, expecting the guys to be setting about preparing dinner. Instead, she found a sight that had shocked her to the core. Long ago, on three sides of the cabin, the group had built a series of short sheds that housed their motorcycles. Since the traveling group had remained in the camp a couple of years ago, they had only brought them out for trips to town once a month or so in turns.

Now, the bikes had all been pulled out and polished until their chrome shone brightly in the setting sun, where they stood in a group waiting for their departure, 12 in all. A lump formed in Tori's throat as she realized how precarious her position was within the group.

Holding her head up, she walked slowly forward into the glow of the campfire that had been built in front of the cabin, just as it had been many nights before. Only this fire held no warmth for her as she stood before Eddie Farrell and looked him in the eye.

Eddie had claimed all her life to be her father, but deep down she had suspected it was a lie. Eddie had been her mentor, teaching her the art of hand to hand combat, but he had also been her nemesis. Often, he would hit her out of the blue or kick her whenever he felt the urge, claiming it would make her tough. She hated him for this.

Tori had often suspected Eddie was jealous that she always chose the company of Henry over him. Now, her actions of the past night felt quite foolish, and she realized Eddie would have been angry with what she had done. She was terrified of Eddie, but she did her best not to show it.

It was too late now for second guessing. As Brian had pushed to make her strong, Eddie had taught her to fight. Each man that now surrounded her had poured what he knew into her empty vessel, and it was time for her to take her place among them.

She stopped squarely in front of the ring leader, her heart pounding wildly inside her chest as she faced him, her chin raised slightly in defiance. She felt a cold breeze on her bare legs. She anticipated his opening swing, and the fight was on as they rolled out of the firelight, each taking jabs and making dodges into the shadowy edges of the night.

Of course, Tori was still lacking experience

in true combat, and he bested her easily, finally knocking her to the ground where she lay on her back looking up at him. He kicked her several times in the ribs in anger, and she wondered why none of the onlookers came to her aid, especially Henry.

Curled in a ball, Tori could feel the searing pain in her side and the tears of agony on her dirty face. Eddie dropped down on top of her, forcing her onto her back once more by sitting on her legs. Reaching down, he ripped her shirt off from the collar, exposing her bare breasts, the new bra nowhere in sight. She screamed in anguish as he leaned over, sinking his teeth deep into the soft flesh of her left breast.

Henry stood silent and watched as Eddie imposed his wrath. As he sat up, Eddie wiped the blood from his mouth, laughing at her cries. "You stupid bitch," he hissed. "Tears are for the weak!" and slapped her across her left cheek with the open face of his right hand.

Tori stared up at him, trying to stop the flood of tears that streamed from her tender blue eyes. He stood up, releasing her legs, and she used her torn shirt to try and stop the flow of blood as it ran down her chest and dripped onto the ground. Pointing a finger in her face, he laughed again and poked the mutilated flesh with a growl, "Now, you will never forget your place."

Reaching down, he grabbed a hand full of her hair and dragged her to her feet, then across to the plain wooden table that stood in the center of their camp. Slamming her back on top of the rough wood, he grabbed the front of her shorts, pulling them open and then off as she struggled to resist him.

Using his fist this time, he punched her, and she fell back against the table and lay still as he finished removing the garments with ease. Dragging her rear to the edge of the table, he opened his own pants and pushed himself inside, snarling with satisfaction as the others looked on in silence.

After a few minutes of work, he decided he needed to make his point clearer, so stepping back he rolled her limp body over, pushing himself into her again, clearly liking his new position much better. When he was finished, he moved away, allowing the other ten men of the group to have a turn at her if they wanted.

As he watched, Henry swallowed back his tears and prayed she wouldn't regain consciousness while they were taking her. Eddie cleaned himself and headed into the cabin to find dinner, but then stopped in front of Henry and said flatly in his deep gravelly voice, "if you ever touch her again, I'll kill her," and continued on his way.

After the others had had their fill, they too moved off into the night to eat and get some sleep. Henry didn't dare touch her or cover her body as she lay in the darkness. He sat on the ground, rocking back and forth next to the dying fire and waited for her to move. The hours passed slowly, and as the sun broke in the eastern sky, a low moan escaped her. Tori shifted, lifting her chest out of the pool of blood that had formed beneath her on the table. A huff of relief escaped Henry's lips as he realized she had survived the night.

Moving slowly, Tori was able to stand, her breast throbbing and her knees weak as she stumbled a few feet, then sank feebly to the ground. She looked up to see Henry staring at her intently, but didn't bother to ask what had happened. She kneeled for several minutes before asking him what she should do. His reply was direct and honest. "Do what he says. Do exactly what he says, when he says, and how, he says. Do it for as long as you can, baby girl. It's the only way you are going to survive."

Tori found little comfort in his advice, and tried to move closer as she reached out to him. She lifted her hand towards him, but he pulled away. "I can't touch you, baby girl," the pain in his deep brown eyes evident; "if I do, he will kill you."

Tori stopped moving, staring at him while

the anger rose inside her. "Then I promise you," she hissed in a low whisper, "someday, I will put him in the ground." Immediately Henry winced, her words tearing at his heart, but deep down, he hoped that it was true.

* * *

"Was I right to share this with you?" Tori asked as she reached a stopping point in her story. Eli was staring out into space. Her words were soft, and she felt exhausted by the experience. He shifted his gaze to her immediately, sitting up straight and nodding profusely.

"Of course," he began in earnest, "But it is getting late, and I am sure that is not all you have to say."

Tori quickly agreed with both statements, and they decided to pick up the next evening, when he was able to return. Rising off the bed, Eli slipped his shoes on, and then moved towards the door, stopping just short of it and turning around.

She stepped closer to him, and he reached out for her hand, grasping it lightly between his fingers anxiously. "I need you to know something before you tell me anymore," his voice cracked and he swallowed hard. "I came here today with the intention of asking you to move in with me."

Tori stared at him blankly; her mind tossed into chaos as she grasped the meaning of his words. "Not with me with me," he stammered, "I mean into my spare room that I have that no one lives in." He paused for a moment, trying to regain his composure. "I mean, I have a spare room in my apartment that is yours whenever you want it or need it, no strings attached." *There, I said it.*

Tori stood another moment before stepping forward and slowly putting her arms around his shoulders in a strong embrace. Eli was slightly shorter than she was, and she leaned down somewhat as she felt his arms move around her waist in return.

Squeezing him firmly, she whispered her

gratitude, and then released him into the hallway, bidding him good night. As he walked down the hall and out the front door, his spirits were strangely high after hearing the gruesome story she had just shared. She had a way of doing that to him though, making him feel almost euphoric just by being close to her. *You sir, are in big trouble*, he thought to himself wryly as he made his way to his car.

A Friend in Deed

Eli arrived early the next day, while Tori sat in a group session. Approaching the door, he could hear the muffled voices as they spoke, and see her through the narrow window made of safety glass. She was seated in the circle of chairs, back straight and chin raised in that stoic, defiant posture of hers.

The sight caused him to chuckle, and he turned towards her room to wait for her. While he walked, he thought about how far she had already come, and yet how far she still had left to go. He had a job to do, but the longer he knew her, the less the job really meant to him.

He had brought a gift for her today, hoping she would not be offended. She had received his last gift in a less than enthusiastic manner, a book of German fairytales, so he felt a bit timid about making a second attempt.

When Tori left the session, she scurried to her room, wanting to brush her hair and prepare for her visitor. She never liked what they had to say in those stupid sessions anyway, and felt somewhat annoyed at even having to attend. Half the time, her mind had wandered over the events of yesterday and her confessions, first to Dr. Carlisle, and then to Eli.

Instead of listening to the speaker, she used the time to plan what she would tell her new friend next. She had 20 years of memories; stories of pain and sadness to share. And while she was now aware this was something she wanted to do, she was still not sure he would be interested by the time they reached the end. Deciding to continue chronologically, she felt tense about what would be next.

To her surprise, Eli was already in her room,

seated in his chair looking out into the garden while he waited. He turned and standing, smiled as soon as she entered the room. Tori could feel her heart pounding, a slight smile teasing the corner of her lips before she could wipe it away. Eli reached down to pick up a single pink rose wrapped in plastic that lay on the table, and handing it to her said simply, "This is for you."

Tori stared down at the bright pink petals in awe for several seconds, not exactly sure what to do with an actual flower. Finally, she raised her eyes and shrugged, which gave Eli a short fit of laughter and he set off into her bathroom to search for something to put water in for the rose.

Returning shortly with a plastic cup of water, he showed her how to unwrap the bloom and stand it in the cup. "Ideally," he explained, "you should trim the stem a small amount so that it can take up water better and last a bit longer."

Tori stared back at him, trying desperately not to allow her excitement at the gift to show. "So," she began, resting the cup on the center of the table, then adjusting the rose inside of it nervously, "you ready for more torture by story, or have you heard enough?" Her face was expressionless, but she genuinely hoped he would be willing to hear more.

Eli agreed to more torture, but only after they had dined. Together, they strolled through the halls towards the cafeteria, Eli making small talk along the way. Tori really liked that about him, the way he would talk to her in a low, whispery voice. She also liked the way he was speaking to her in French right now. Good practice he called it. On the inside, she was beaming with joy and could not have cared less if the whole room noticed them and stared.

After their meal, they made a pass through the garden, and Tori took the opportunity to show off a little by pointing out some of the bird species for him. Eli smiled wistfully, lightly grasping the fingers of her hand as it hung next to his for a moment before he released her. As they stood only inches apart, he had suddenly realized he was in a dangerous place at this moment. He reluctantly took a step back before he was tempted to kiss her.

Sensing his discomfort, a scowl flittered across her features before she made her way back to the glass door and then her room in silence. She felt confused by his actions, as if she were lost, trapped between all that had happened to her and all the things she didn't understand.

When they arrived back in the safety of her quarters, Tori assumed they would follow the ritual of the day before, closing the door and slipping off her shoes to sit on the bed, grasping her pillow. This time, however, Eli hesitated, "I'm not sure I should sit on the bed with you. Maybe we should sit in chairs, or at least I should . . ." he let his words fade as he spoke.

Unsure how to take the change in his behavior, Tori blinked for a moment, then indicated her agreement by wafting her hand towards one of the empty seats. Eli grabbed the closest one and sat in it next to her bed so that he could hear, but was not in too compromising of a position.

Tori first asked if he had any questions about what he had heard so far, and to her surprise he did ask for clarification on several points. Such as, had she ever been to town while the group lived in the camp? Tori explained that she had never been anywhere, but the camp prior to their departure and the world was strictly maps and pictures in books up to that point. She knew that it existed, but had never experienced any of it.

"So you had a lot of books then?" he inquired next.

"Oh yes," Tori replied. "The guys would go into town at least once every other month or so to pick up supplies. They always brought back new books for me on those trips, books for lessons and for me to read." Her appetite for the written word was insatiable.

Listening while she spoke, Eli noticed the book he had given her on the floor next to her bed, a slip of paper sticking out from the pages. *A bookmark perhaps?* The thought made him smile, *maybe she liked my gift after all.*

"They had built a bookcase along one wall of the cabin to hold all my books," she continued,

"And it broke my heart when we left. I was made to choose only one to take with me, and after that, if I acquired a new book, the old one had to be left behind." Her sadness was apparent as she spoke. Eli only nodded, bracing himself emotionally to hear whatever she was going to tell him next.

Tori had already decided to avoid being too graphic with Eli, and she hoped she would be able to stick to that plan. Picking up on the same day she left off on, she explained how Henry's best friend, Anthony Livingstone had stepped up to take his place now that he had been forbidden to touch her.

Of course, this was an issue for Tori, as having lived with the group of men her entire life, there were a couple of them she really did not like, and Tony was one of them. Of course, it never occurred to her that the feeling was mutual, and he only tended to her now because Henry had asked him to.

So basically, Tori sat in angry silence as Tony tended her wounds and helped her clean herself up. The bite on her breast was swollen and red, as the deep puncture wounds made it easy to trace the outline of Eddie's mouth. After cleaning it, Tony covered it with a dressing so that she could wear the bra and other clothing that she had been given. Tony's face showed no sympathy as she gingerly washed her nether regions with the water he warmed for her. "You still got a lot to learn," he muttered as he put the first aid kit away, tossing her clothes onto the table next to her.

Eddie's Girl

The Dragons spent three more days in their bush camp before hitting the road. Tori needed that time to become acclimatized to her new role within the group, no longer the pupil, now an intern. Tony made sure she wore all of the clothing she was given, which felt constrictive and cumbersome as she donned the attire she had seen on the other Dragons for years.

The boots felt like lead weights on her feet, and the leather jacket was heavy across her shoulders. However, any remark she made in disagreement over what was expected of her was handled with a heavy retribution and she quickly learned to be silent about her discomfort.

Once she had been cleaned up and was appropriately dressed, Eddie announced he had a gift for her, and presented her with a long, flat and narrow, plain white box. Tori, feeling beaten but not broken, snatched the box from him and lifted the lid.

Inside, there lay a silver six inch OTF switchblade knife with the letters T-O-R-I engraved in the handle. She stared blankly at the knife, her mind sifting through the training he had given her over the last couple of years, until she reached the part about knives, and she pushed to lever to watch the blade pop out the end, and then returned it to its hidden state.

Eddie had taught her how to hold one, although her hand had been too clumsy to do a good job at the time. He had taught her anatomy and where to put the knife to be most effective depending on whether she wanted to wound or kill the person she was attacking. She knew every major artery in the body and how to sever it with just such a weapon. Back then, she had never understood the purpose of those lessons.

A cold chill ran through her under the hot afternoon sun as she realized they were actually expecting her to use the sharpened tool. Looking up at the circle of faces that had formed around her, the men were now strangers to her, their motives clear. Tori was no longer a child, and she would take her place among them whether she wanted to or not.

Closing the box, she stepped through the ring and walked away from the camp, headed along the trail until she reached her favorite spot. Wearing the bulky clothes, she did not have the energy to make the climb, so she slumped down at the base of the tree, her back against the trunk, and stared down into the valley forest below.

She wanted to cry, but the tears refused to come. Feeling the weight of the skin on her face, she sat in silence, not really thinking about anything. Eventually, Tony came up and dropped down on the ground beside her. She cut her eyes over to give him a menacing look, but said nothing.

"You better get that attitude in check," he

warned her gruffly, pointing a finger at her in return. "I told Henry I would look out for you and I intend to do that, but I'm not gonna stop what you got comin' to you." He paused for a breath while she shifted her gaze back to the scene below.

Continuing, he rasped, "You're in a whole new world now. You're not a full member, but Eddie wants you to be. That is your purpose. That is why you exist. Eddie owns you, and you'll do what he says or you'll pay the price. Now, get up and get back to camp at a reasonable hour." Standing, he did not wait for her. Tori sat for some time longer, considering his words, the anger simmering inside of her.

As the sun made its way across the sky, the words 'reasonable hour' echoed in her ear. Not wanting a full repeat of the night before, she stood reluctantly and opened Eddie's gift once more. Tossing the box onto the ground, she slipped the knife into her pocket and made her way back to the cabin.

As soon as she arrived, it was clear her definition of 'reasonable' was somewhat different than what Eddie had in mind. Walking up to her while shaking his head, he was mumbling how she always had been a stubborn girl. Then he calmly reached up, poking the patch of tender skin that Tony had dressed with clean gauze just that morning. Stepping back, Tori covered the spot with her right hand, the stabs of pain intense. Her reaction made Eddie grin as he walked away.

The Dragons set about preparing dinner as usual, but Tori knew that usual was gone forever. She could feel the guys looking at her, watching her as she moved, and it made her uncomfortable. She had no friends now as none of them could be trusted. She caught a glimpse of Henry, who was keeping to the edge of the group to avoid her, and she felt a wave of guilt twinge inside her. Henry had once been a respected member of the Dragons. Because of her, he had lost his position, and that brought her immense pain.

Tori did her best to lie low while the meal was prepared and consumed. She caught bits and pieces of reference to the events of the night before in the conversation, and she was almost certain the group members were looking for an encore. Another fire was built, and she ate her meat and potato in silence while crouching next to the flickering flames.

She didn't like the site of it, knowing it meant trouble having a fire so many nights in a row. While the group ate, they only spoke at sporadic intervals. After most of them had finished, it was decided they needed to have a little contest—battle of the Silver they called it.

Immediately, Tori knew this was going to be some kind of drinking game, which was a common event on fire nights. She had seen nights like this many times in the past, and a surge of apprehension rose inside her chest.

Drinking games meant there would be loud boisterous voices, old stories would be retold, and most of them would be sloppy drunk well before midnight. On occasion, fights would break out, and for that reason, she would almost always slip off to the safety of her hammock as soon as she had eaten. She would then spend the night watching and listening from afar. Remaining crouched by the fire, she considered trying to slip away as usual, but a hand clamped down on her shoulder, and she knew tonight there was no escape.

The group descended into general chaos with bottles being brought out from all over the camp, and a chair was placed at the table where she had awoken naked, earlier in the day. She was instructed to sit. Tori stood, staring at seat as if it were a rabid dog, and a hand came across to poke the tender spot on her chest. Startled, Tori's hand shot up to protect the injury, and she turned, surprised to see it was Red who had done the poking.

Gerald Farrell, or Red as he was called, was Eddie's twin brother. They were identical twins, although they were nothing alike. Eddie was the leader of the pair, and Red was the follower. They had been inseparable through the years. They went to school together, they joined the marines together, they rode together. Clenching her jaw, Tori swore to herself they were going to die together as she fingered the new knife in her pocket.

Red indicated the metal stand and again

instructed her to sit. After a brief look around the group, Tori stepped forward and took a seat. As she did so, she noticed that Henry had turned his back and was walking away, headed North in the direction of her favorite tree. She would have given anything to have been walking with him. He tramped slowly, his footsteps thumping heavily, and she knew her dearest friend was now in purgatory and could not bear watch what was surely awaiting her as the night wore on.

Tori sat in the chair while five shot glasses were placed on the table in front of her, and she could feel her palms begin to sweat. She had seen the guys drink many times, but she herself had never tasted alcohol. As the glasses were filled she was given the rules, which made no sense what so ever, and then she was told to drink. Nervously, her left hand shaking as she reached out, she picked up the first glass and tried to keep it from spilling.

Her right hand slipping back into the pocket and stroked the knife. Raising the glass to her face, the stench of the brew burning her nose, she took a small sip of the vile liquid and almost dropped the glass in her lap as she coughed. The group burst into laughter at her feeble attempt and Tori could feel her face growing crimson in a mixture of embarrassment and rage.

David grabbed another chair and positioned himself beside her, designating himself as her coach. Taking the second shot, he demonstrated how to slam the drink down, instructing her not to taste it. Giving her an encouraging slap on the back, he waited for her to give it another try. Still stroking the knife, Tori manage to get some of the third shot down, while most of it spilled down her front and onto her folded legs.

Still playing the role of coach, Dave gave her a brief recap on the directions along with an all inspiring, you can do it fist pump. Tori managed to down the fourth and fifth glasses, proclaiming loudly, "that's not even all the same shit," which was met with a loud cheer from the group as the glasses were refilled.

Staring at the line, she could see that one of the glasses was a clear liquid, like water with almost no odor. Three were various shades of gold, and the last looked like a deep auburn.

This time, she reached for the clear glass, thinking the color could make a difference in the taste, and managed to get the drink down with crossed eyes and nose wrinkled in disgust. It was at that point she realized that the contest was being judged based on the expression on her face as she drank. Still stroking the knife, she downed the next four in quick succession, trying not to make a face as best she could. This only made the group laugh harder as they filled the glasses again.

While she sat staring at the process, Tori suddenly felt overly warm, and longed to remove the jacket. However, she knew by doing so, she would no longer have possession of the knife she intended to use to defend herself. She chewed on her lower lip, noticing it tingled as she bit on it.

After several minutes, Tori ran her tongue over her top lip a few times and reached for the first glass in the row, this time downing it quickly, slamming the empty back in place on the table. She swallowed the next four just as easily, and a loud cheer went up from the group as she stood up and proclaimed herself the winner, intending to cut for her bunk at that point.

Heading her off, Eddie stepped up and asked if she were ready to take her clothes off yet. Tori laughed out loud at his request, pointing out she never wanted to have them on in the first place, and dropped the jacket to the ground. The alcohol had hit her quickly, and her mind had become a mess of confused thoughts and conflicting ideas.

She could feel hands groping her and tried to push them away, grasping at the memory of resisting. She noticed several of the guys had taken up spots around the edge of the firelight and now sat on the ground watching the spectacle in amusement. Trying to hold on to her sober self, Tori put her finger in Eddie's face, "you aren't going to touch me tonight," in the most menacing voice she could muster.

"Oh yeah?" he countered with a snort, "You always were a stubborn little bitch." He pushed up against her, forcing her to backpedal until she reached the table, bumping into it with her rear end. The glasses were gone, and a tube now lay on the table. She could barely make out the giant K on the front of it through her swirling vision. "Take your clothes off, Tori," he commanded.

Tori realized now she had removed the jacket and the knife was gone. Unable to give up, she took a swing at him while hands grabbed her from both sides, forcing her down onto the flat surface, lying face up. She began to scream obscenities at them as they pulled off her boots and removed the lower half of her clothing.

She could feel a sting on her upper left bicep and flailed wildly trying to push them off to no avail. Once her lower body was bare, she was rolled over, face down on the table, and she could feel her hands and ankles being bound. She pulled profusely with her right hand, but then realized that the two hands were now connected somehow under the table, as pulling with one only forced the other underneath.

While she struggled with her hands, trying to figure out how to free herself, she could feel fingers rubbing and touching her in places nothing ever belonged, and a cold oozing feeling running down the crack of her rear end. As Eddie positioned himself, then forced his way inside, she grabbed the edges of the table, unable to scream, as if her lungs had clamped shut in the agony.

Reaching forward, he grabbed the back of her hair and lifted her face off the table so he could reach her better. Turning her face, he bit her on the ear and hissed, "You're my girl, you stupid bitch, and you always will be." As he worked and moaned, Tori stopped resisting, her mind and body suddenly frozen in helplessness, and a few moments later the blessed blackness fell.

Win or Lose

The next morning, Tori awoke lying across the table much the way she had been the day before. This time, a short rope hung from her left wrist, the burn on the right matching it, a tell-tale sign of what had occurred. As she sat up, her body ached, and a wave of nausea sent her spewing vomit on the ground as she collapsed to her knees.

"Well, that's pretty disgusting," remarked Tony as he walked up, first aid kit in hand. Getting to her feet, she sat on the table, and he began to inspect her wounds. When she remarked that she felt awkward with the bottom half of her body naked, Tony replied, "Doesn't matter, this has to come off too," as he lifted her shirt off over her head and began unstrapping the bra.

Tori didn't bother to resist, and just sat fully naked as he removed the dressing from her breast and examined the marks closely. While he worked, he began to talk, and through the pounding headache, Tori realized she was about to get a lecture.

"You realize you can't win. Not even close. There are eleven of us not counting Henry. Now, I know you're strong, and you've worked hard all your life doing whatever we asked you to do. And we both know you can fight—I have seen you, and you are actually pretty good. But you're not gonna win. Not against all of us." Finishing the bite, he moved on to the fresh burn mark that was blistering up on her left bicep.

"Take this, for example," he indicated the injury, "this is what you get when you fight. You get hurt, and you still lose." He paused for a few minutes to get her a bottle of water, and she began to sip on it slowly. The morning sun hurt her eyes, and he could see she was suffering. Normally he wouldn't give a rat's ass if she suffered. He welcomed it, in fact, having hated her since the beginning.

"Why the hell are you so stubborn?" he asked pointedly. "You always got a hard head, like you're gonna get your way. Henry spoiled you for too long, I think, letting you have your way." Tori made no effort to reply and continued to drink the water.

Tony gave a long sigh, running his fingers through his short blond hair as he stared off into the distance. He could tell taking care of her was going to be harder than he thought if she didn't get some sense knocked into her soon. Cutting his eyes to look at her, she was staring down at the bottle.

"Tell me what you want then," she muttered.

"What I want? It's not about what I want. It's about what Eddie wants. Eddie's in charge. You gotta do what he wants. Look Tori, you're a smart girl, we both know that. Smart as they come, I mean that's why you're here. But you gotta use your head and not pick fights you can't win. You gotta do what you gotta do." He began waving his hands to add emphasis to his words.

"See, we all gotta do what we gotta do. When we get back on the road, you gotta know your job, and this," he pointed between her legs, "this is your job. As far as anyone outside is ever gonna know, it's your only job. Eddie's gonna give you other jobs, and them jobs are a secret, a secret you guard with your life."

Tori stared at him in a state of confusion. Disgusted, he continued to clean her wounds in silence. When he was finished, he handed her the second set of clothes that had been purchased for her. "Now, you have to go ask Eddie for permission to go to the creek to wash your other set. He ain't gonna like that. On the road, gotta take care of your clothes or go dirty."

Tori slipped on the lace panties and winced as they rubbed against her raw posterior. She was sore from last night, and suddenly very glad she had not been awake for the majority of it despite the hangover. After putting on the rest of her uniform, she looked down into her boots to make sure she hadn't picked up any creepy crawlies and turning them upside down, banged them against the table before sticking her foot in, just as she had seen the guys do many times. Tony watched as she got dressed, and for an instant his expression softened, as if he actually felt sorry for her, being alone with twelve men all these years.

Tori picked up her wad of soiled clothing and sighed. Tony was right, and she knew it. Henry had always helped her out with her clothes, and she actually had taken pretty good care of her three or four pair of shorts, her sandals, and her shirts until her chest exploded, and they didn't fit anymore.

They only made trips down to the creek to wash and get water on schedule, so asking for a special trip was going to be rough. She could see Eddie over under a tree, working on his bike, getting ready for their trip. Trudging slowly, she practiced in her head what she was going to say, trying to be meek and submissive, and prayed he wouldn't poke her tender breast again.

With soft footsteps, Tori stopped next to Eddie and waited. He stood, giving her a look up and down, wrench in hand. She suspected that he knew what she wanted, even before she asked. "May we please go down to the creek so I can wash my clothes," she spoke in a small timid voice he had never heard before. He smiled to himself at her attempt to grovel. She would have to do a better job, and she knew it.

"You know we are leaving tomorrow or the next day," he replied, "You be a good girl and we will make a trip for you before we head out. Right now, sit down here with me and let's get these bikes tuned up for the journey."

That's a strange request, Tori thought as she dropped her load of garments next to the tree. She never spent spare time working with Eddie. She had always been Henry's girl, and would prefer to be on the other side of the compound strumming his guitar right now. But things had changed, and she knew she was going to have to get with the program if she were going to survive.

Kneeling down next to his small box of tools, Tori wrinkled her nose at the grease and poked a few of the items with one finger.

"You know what any of them are?" Eddie asked in a more cheerful tone than he typically used with her.

"No," she gave a flat, noncommittal response.

"Well then, its time you learned," his voice became curt at her surliness, "this is a wrench," he said waving the tool at her, and proceeded to explain what he was doing and why.

Tori listened intently, trying harder to please him. Moving through the steps of the procedure, she began to ask questions, but she could tell it was irritating him, so she tried to be quiet. A short time later, curiosity got the better of her again, and she posed another query, this time receiving a glare of contempt at her lack of knowledge. For a moment, she thought he was going to strike her, and she rocked back on her heels to avoid the blow.

"Hey guys," Henry made his presence known. "I need to have a word with Eddie for a minute, baby girl. Why don't you grab your stuff here and put it away, and you can come back and learn more about motorcycles after lunch." Tori could see the anger in Eddie's eyes, and for a moment she was too scared to move, not knowing what to do. Eventually, she seized the pile and headed towards the cabin, actually relieved the lesson was over.

When she arrived at the small structure, she went about putting together a light lunch for herself of meat and cheese, and had started making a second for Henry before she realized it really wasn't her place anymore to do so. *Everything is so messed up now*, she lamented to herself.

She completed the second meal and wrapped it for later, and then began nibbling at hers. While she ate, other members of the group came in and also had a bite to eat. None of them spoke to her, and she shifted uncomfortably as they moved around behind her, laughing and joking with each other, leaving her to feel forlorn and alone.

Three of the guys had gone hunting, and they returned with the meat for the night's dinner. In the midst of their haul, they had captured an anaconda, about 5 feet in length. Normally, she would have been very pleased, as she loved the taste of the snake meat. With the events of the past few days, Tori no longer felt joy or cared about what there was to eat. Reluctantly, she set about helping them clean the carcass and prepare it to be cooked.

While they worked, Henry and Eddie made their way up the hill. Henry's face was calm, but Eddie looked cross, his brow furrowed in an angry scowl. Seeing the second lunch she had prepared, he barked some obscenities, assuming it had been for Henry.

Henry looked down at the offering, then over at the girl, who shook her head and pointing at Eddie, "no, it's for you," she tried to cover for her blunder. Feeling overly tired, Tori excused herself from the cleaning party by rinsing her hands, and heading towards her hammock.

Tori's hammock hung in a special place amongst the trees away from the other guys, in a more secluded location. It had been set lower to the ground, as she had been shorter when Henry put it up for her. As she laid in it now, her rear end almost dragging the dirt, and she realized she must have been lighter the last time she lay in it, as well.

Thinking back, she could not remember how long it had been since she had started sleeping in Henry's bunk with him. She guessed it must have been a couple of years, when the rest of the group had remained in the camp instead of heading back out.

Lying in the hammock, slowly gliding back and forth, she drifted between awake and asleep, considering how things had changed in the last few days. Eddie had always claimed to be her father, but she had never really believed that. Deep down, she had once thought Henry was. Now she knew that neither man could be.

Eddie isn't my father, she told herself with conviction. *Fathers don't rape their little girls.* She put her face into her hands as if to cry, but again, no tears would come. *"Tears are for the weak"* Eddie had said.

Well, I'm not weak. The advice Tony had given her flowed through her mind, *"don't pick fights you can't win."* There had to be something wrong with that logic; she knew it in her gut.

Turning on her side, she curled into a ball, rocking back and forth, the hammock almost dragging the earth below. *So if there is no fight, there is no win or lose... You have to learn your job... This is your job.*

Swinging back and forth, Tori finally fell asleep. When she awoke, the sun was low in the sky. Realizing it was now past the 'reasonable' time she should have rejoined the group, she felt she should have been worried. She wasn't.

Grabbing her brush out of her small stash of personal items, Tori brushed out her long black tresses. Giving herself a quick once over to make sure her appearance was in order, she left her secluded spot and headed for the cabin, her hips swaying as she walked.

Approaching the gathering, she could see from Eddie's posture he was pissed. Choosing to ignore him, she made her way around the outer ring, being sure to reach out and touch anyone and everyone who came close to her, her fingers sliding lightly down backs and across chests as she moved from man to man.

Stopping in front of David, who was sitting in a chair across from the cabin door, she leaned over so that her rear end stuck out noticeably, placing her arm ever so carelessly on his shoulder and cooed, "So hun, who actually won last night's game?" She could see him swallow as he looked down her shirt.

For a moment, his eyes were an empty, lost stare. So, trying to be helpful, Tori shifted so that her rear end twitched, and indicated the size of a shot glass with her fingers, "You know, who had the tastiest drink?" she inquired using a soft little voice that dripped with honey.

Paul, who was standing nearby, jumped in practically shouting, "I won. You want some now?"

Tori straightened, turning to place her hand

on his chest, "Sure Pauly, I'd like that," she fussed over him. Immediately he scampered away to find his bottle of liquid sunshine.

Tori turned to see Eddie and Henry standing next to each other about 15 feet from her. Eddie's face was like stone, while Henry's mouth stood half open in awe. She may never have seen a woman in action, but Tori had read enough about them.

I know what I can do to a man if I want to; she thought to herself as she blew Eddie a kiss. Then, Paul was back with a bottle of rum. Unscrewing the cap, Tori turned the bottle up, surprised at how easy it was to swig knowing how awful it was going to taste. After three swallows, she returned the cap, purring to him while tapping the bottle, "You shouldn't get too far away with that."

The next few minutes there was a flurry of activity as dinner was prepared, and the fire was lit. Tori didn't help much this evening, as she usually did, spending most of the time swinging her hair around and looking for opportunities to lean against someone. Paul followed her around like a lost puppy, so she made sure to stroke his ego often.

As soon as the meat was ready, the group began to eat. Tori managed to eat a small plate as well, even though her stomach had turned to knots now that her plan was in action. Her palms had begun to grow sweaty as she realized what she was going to do next. She surveyed the group, wanting to wait on starting the main event until everyone had finished their meal.

Seeing Henry, he made a motion to her and she stepped over close enough to speak, but instead of letting him talk, she simply gave him a quiet warning, "You should take off now, Love. You're not gonna want to be here for this one either." Henry stared into her crystal blue eyes, considering her words for a moment, and then moving to obey slipped away into the night.

Finding Paul, Tori drank another five or six swallows of the rum, but kept the bottle, thanking him with a peck on the cheek. *It's almost show time.* Taking a few cleansing breaths, she could see Eddie sitting on the ground, leaning with his back square against the side of the cabin. *It's now or never;* Tori thought to herself as she made a beeline for him.

Walking straight up, she swung her leg over his so she could sit on his lap straddling him, face to face. When she plunked down, he sat up, grabbing both of her upper arms, "What the hell are you doing?"

Tori cackled, opening the bottle for another swig, then teased, "I thought this is what you wanted . . ." He released her arms, leaning back in surprise, so she leaned in closer and whispered loudly, "Can I take my clothes off now?"

Eddie immediately shoved her off his lap and jumped to his feet. Not losing a beat, Tori sprang up beside him and stepped towards him. To her surprise, he backed away, and for a moment she was completely confused what to do next. Then she began to laugh. Eddie only liked it when she put up a fight. But she had come too far to back out now, so she swung around looking at the rest of the group.

"Well, does anyone else wanna fuck?" Luckily, there was no shortage of volunteers, and she began to pull off her boots first, then her jeans, remembering to fold up each item as it came off and set it aside so it would be cleanish for her the next day.

To Tell or Not to Tell

Eli sat in stunned silence as Tori stopped speaking. Her face was as expressionless as ever, so he could not tell how she felt about what she had just revealed, but he honestly hoped she was joking. "So, you just went ahead and had sex with all of them that night?" he asked anxiously.

"Yeah," Tori answered with a shrug, "Well, I don't really think it was all of them, I really don't know for sure. Some of them I guess. All I know is, I won that night, more or less. Of course, Eddie had gone stomping out into the jungle and didn't come back until the next day. And when he did, there was hell to pay, which I guess I will tell you about tomorrow."

"No," Eli demanded, "You will tell me now." Tori stared at him blankly, so he continued. "Look, I have listened patiently this whole time while you described how 'bad' your life was and now you're sitting here saying you just spread your legs for the whole crew like it was no big deal? I don't get it Tori, what the hell is wrong with you?"

His words cut deep, and she gasped for air as if she had been kicked in the gut. Standing, she moved to the far corner, where the left and back walls met, and leaned against it, rocking slightly. "I don't know what's wrong with me," she finally stammered, "Maybe you should just go now."

"Yeah well, maybe I should." Eli left without another word, leaving the door open, and Tori standing in the corner, her whole body beginning to tremble.

But I won that night; she thought to herself, over and over, until an orderly called through the doorway, "Hey, lights out in 5."

Tori didn't give any indication she had heard him, so he stepped into the room, grabbing her shoulder to get her attention. Blinded by rage, she reached with her left hand and captured the offending digits, swung around and began hitting him with her right fist. Hearing the commotion and the man's cries for help, the patient across the hall looked in before running down the passage screaming for assistance.

A second orderly ran to her room, stopping at the door completely frozen at the sight. Finally, a third was able to push past him, and Tori felt the leads of the Taser pierce her skin, immediately followed by excruciating pain. Releasing her victim, she tried to comply with their demands.

*   *   *

Eli climbed into his car, tossing his jacket into the passenger seat in disgust, he could already feel regret creeping up his spine. Tori had been nothing but honest and trusting of him, and he had no right to speak to her that way. He was growing impatient, waiting for her to get to the part that mattered to him and the investigation.

Cursing his actions, he slammed his palms

into the steering wheel and then propped his forehead against it. He was still sitting there when his cell phone buzzed in his pocket. Fumbling to retrieve the device, he flipped it open and chirped a simple, "Hello?"

"Did you come to visit Tori today?" an angry voice demanded. Eli was pretty sure it was Dr. Carlisle.

"Yeah, sure, I just left, in fact," he answered smoothly, trying not sound excited, "Haven't even made it out of the parking lot yet."

"Well, if that's the case we need you back inside *right now*." The doctor was practically shouting and hung up before Eli could even respond.

Trying to remain calm, Eli closed his flip phone and looked back at the front of the building. From his car everything looked fine. For a moment, he considered starting the engine and heading home, then thought better of it and climbed out. Leaving his jacket in the front seat, he trotted back up to the building and through the front door while straightening his tie.

Inside everything was chaos. Patients were scurrying around the hallways, chatter buzzing all over the place. An orderly was going down the hall trying to get patients back into their rooms, to no avail. An alarm was sounding, and red lights were blinking at intervals down the hall.

The sight sent Eli's heart pounding into overdrive, and he raced down the hall towards her room. When he arrived, he covered his mouth in shock, and he could feel the tears burn as they poured down his face. *This is my fault,* he admonished himself.

On the floor, an orderly was receiving medical attention, blood covering his face. Sidling into the room, he could see bits of blood splatter on the wall, the chair, the bed, everywhere he looked. Tori, however, was nowhere in sight.

Shuffling back out into the hall, he could see Dr. Carlisle at the far end. Jogging towards him, Eli had to dodge patients who refused to comply with the numerous people now trying to get everyone back into their rooms. "Where is she?" he demanded as soon as he reached the doctor.

"She is over in the next wing. Let's go." They walked as fast as they dared through the unruly halls, Dr. Carlisle's lip twitching in anger. As they left the minimum security level of the hospital, he slowed enough for Eli to catch up beside him, "What were you and Tori talking about before you left?"

Not getting any type of reply, the doctor stopped, turning to face the other man squarely. "Look, this is really important right now. Yesterday, I thought I was making a serious break through with this girl. And then tonight she beats an orderly senseless, right after you left. You weren't having sex with her were you?"

"Hell no!" Eli's reply was instantaneous, but the doctor wasn't buying it. *Why would he even think that we were?* Eli wondered incredulously.

Pursing his lips tightly, Dr. Carlisle turned and continued walking towards the swinging doors at the end of the hallway. "You know, if you weren't a Federal Agent you wouldn't even be in this place, coming and going as you please. You better figure out what you have to tell us, because, at this moment; that girl's life could depend on it. Wait here!" Eli stopped as commanded, watching as the doctor disappeared into one of the rooms down the hall.

Eli stood nervously squirming, shifting his weight from one foot to the other. *Oh, my god, this is out of control... I can't even tell when I am pretending anymore.... This wasn't part of the plan.... Please, dear god, please let her be ok....* His thoughts began to run in circles as he waited. Finally, the doctor reappeared, looking calmer. "Can I see her?" Eli begged while trying to appear as calm as the doctor.

"Maybe later," the older man replied. "Right now, you and I need to go to my office and have a nice long chat."

As they walked, Eli suddenly felt as if he were going to be in real trouble once the doctor heard what he had to say, but he obediently followed in silence. Once arriving, Eli sat in one of the leather covered chairs on the patient side of the desk, while Dr. Carlisle took a seat in his oversized desk chair.

Leaning back, the doctor sat for a moment holding his hands about chest high, palms facing each other, allowing his fingers to bounce off one another lightly. "You seem nervous," the doctor stated flatly, "Tori is being examined as we speak. If there has been any misconduct on your part—"

"Of course I am nervous; something has just happened with someone I care for very much," Eli interrupted the doctor, his voice raised with irritation while thinking, *My god, is that the truth?* Out loud he continued, "And I already told you, we weren't doing anything wrong. We were talking, period, that's it." He pushed his hands away from his body to emphasize there being nothing inappropriate with anything that had passed between them.

On the inside, he only wished that were true. Suddenly, Eli was feeling very guilty about lying to Tori and to the doctor, who genuinely seemed interested in helping her. *This is like a sick joke we are playing on her, kicking her when she is down.*

"All right," Dr. Carlisle pulled his chair up to his desk, grabbing a pen and his yellow tablet. "I want you to tell me every conversation you can remember for the last 48 hours. Everything she said, and everything you said."

Eli sat for a moment trying to decide if he were really going to go through with this. *This whole set up was to get information from her, but so far I haven't gotten anything useful. Maybe we should just make an excuse, pull the girl out and go another route before someone really gets hurt.* Deep down Eli knew this could be Tori's only chance at a different life, a better life.

Taking a deep breath, he started with finding Tori sitting at the fountain and continued from there. As he spoke, his tongue felt dry and swollen, and he prayed to god he was doing the right thing.

Can't Fool Me

Three days later, Tori sat in the same exact seat that Eli had occupied in Dr. Carlisle's office. The doctor was patiently waiting for her to begin explaining her story to him, as she had done for Eli. She was angry at Eli for breaking her confidence and ashamed he had caught her, more or less, in a lie. Lastly, she was completely mortified that an innocent man could have been seriously injured or killed because of her.

Tori shifted in her chair, trying to figure out exactly what to say, not knowing what the doctor even actually knew. Finally, she asked, "Is there any way the three of us could meet together? I really would like to speak to him before I try to go any further with this whole situation."

The doctor bit the tip of his pen for a moment, considering her request. "Let me call him, see if he can meet with us." Lifting his phone, the doctor began to dial Eli's number with the end of the writing device.

Tori sat playing with her fingers while she waited, considering the possible outcomes of the call. *One, Eli could come and pronounce me a lying whore. Two, Eli could come and laugh in my face at my stupidity. Three . . .* the doctor hung up the phone. "It will take him about half an hour to get here. Let's go have a quick lunch while we wait."

The doctor stood and waited for her to join him at the door. Reluctantly, Tori rose from her chair and together they walked down the hall. Fortunately, it was just before 11 am, so the traffic in the cafeteria was still light. The doctor smiled and talked to the ladies behind the counter while they were gathering their items. Tori kept her head down, trying not to be noticed.

Once they were seated, the two of them ate

without conversation. The doctor made a mental note of the food the girl had chosen, noticing it was all meat, fruit and vegetable. No pasta and no bread. She also drank water, which he felt was also somewhat odd. He allowed her to eat in peace, then, dumping their dirty trays, they headed back to his office. When they arrived, Eli was waiting outside the door.

As soon as he saw them coming, the dark haired man jumped up from his chair. A wide smile burst across his face, and he could not contain himself as she drew close, reaching out and grabbing her for a hug and grateful she accepted his affectionate gesture.

Eli had not been allowed to speak to or see her after his visit with the doctor. In fact, basically all he had been told was, she is fine, and go away. He had hardly slept since. Holding her now, he didn't want to let go, so he just stood for a moment, rocking side to side, with her body pressed against his. Tori did not resist, but she did not return the hug either, so the doctor cleared his throat loudly, indicating it was time to go into his office and begin.

Tori chose the chair on the far side of the pair, furthest from the door. Taking her seat, she felt completely unnerved. When everyone was settled in, the doctor indicated this was now Tori's show, so to speak, and allowed her to take the lead. She thought for a moment before she began in a shaky voice.

"Well, I just really wasn't sure what I should say. I mean; I am not even sure exactly what all Eli has told you," she indicated the doctor with her right hand, "or anything like that. So, basically that's what I need to know first. Where do we stand?"

Eli smiled supportively, reassuring her the best he could. He explained that he had told the doctor everything that each of them had said; start to finish, and even made sure to apologize for the things he had said that had hurt her so deeply, pushing her over the edge.

Tori's expression transformed into one of surprise. "No Eli, it wasn't what you said that made me . . ." her voice drifted away and she took a deep breath. "I did things I shouldn't have. And it's not your fault. It's mine. I was telling you my story, and I was trying to be honest, and suddenly, I just couldn't take it. I didn't want to tell you the truth. I didn't want it *to be* the truth. I'm sorry." Staring at her hands, she sat waiting for one of them to comment, but neither of the men spoke, waiting for her to continue.

"When I said that I won that day, I lied. I didn't win. Eddie loved the idea of my 'giving myself' to the group. So, he let me take my clothes off, and then things pretty much went the same as they had the two nights before. I mean; I didn't resist and I let them do what they wanted, but what they wanted hurt really bad and I never enjoyed any of it or wanted it to begin with. It became like a game between us, and I played my part. That's it, and that's how it was."

She took a deep breath before she finished. "All the years I was with them, I never wanted it to be like that, but I couldn't do anything about it, so I drank whenever I could and tried to pretend like I didn't care... but I did care. And that isn't even the worst part of what they made me do." She stopped there, unable to go on.

The two men sat in silence, waiting for her to recover and go on, but she didn't. Finally, the doctor asked in a soothing tone, "Would you like to wait, continue this at a later time?"

Tori looked across the desk at him, and then turned to peek at Eli before dropping her gaze back to her lap. Drawing a deep breath, she confessed, "It won't matter when we talk about it. It's bad. It's really bad. I really don't know if I can tell you anymore. I think I'm done." They couldn't see the blood on her hands, but she knew it was there.

"But you have to." Eli stated flatly, and Tori looked up in surprise. "I mean, you're not going to get better if you don't deal with this." He tried to cover his blunder. *I am going to lose*, he thought to himself. *No matter what I do from here on, I am going to lose.*

"But there's so much," she stammered. "Is any part better than another? Can I just skip some? I could just keep going straight through, but it hurts so much. I just don't want to."

"I think you need a break then," the doctor interjected. "I tell you what. Agent Founder, you are welcome to spend time here, of course, but keep it professional. I have to admit, I think the social interaction is doing as much for her as the therapy. Just remember to keep me informed— either Tori tells me, or you tell me, but I need to be up on what's going on in that head of hers if I am going to help her. And you, young lady—the next time you are feeling any aggressive anything, you come straight to me. We can't have you beating up staff members at bed time anymore."

"Is he ok?" she asked meekly.

"He's fine." The doctor answered with a small grin. "You bloodied him up pretty good, but it comes with the job. You kind of have to expect it sometimes working in a place like this. Now get out of here."

Tori and Eli left the office together and made their way to the fountain. Sitting on the edge, her mind began to relax, and a random thought popped into her head. "You really have a brother named Joe?"

Surprised, Eli responded with a chuckle, "Yeah, I actually do have a brother named Joe. I'm surprised you remember me telling you that. When I was talking to you, trying to get you to talk, and you just sat there."

"Why would you be surprised? I was listening after all. I just wonder what it's like to have brothers or sisters or anything like that. I don't really have any family; I guess. Eddie would tell people he was my father, other people believed him, but not me. I think he was making it up just to have something to say. So, I don't really have a family." She rambled a bit, but Eli didn't mind.

"You have a family, Tori." Eli corrected her. "And you're right, Eddie wasn't your father. We did a DNA profile on you versus everyone who was in the house and we got no matches of any sort. So we will keep looking."

"How does that work exactly? The DNA profile thing," Tori wondered aloud.

Eli explained to her how they could take a

sample from her and any other person and run a comparison to find out if they are related in any way. "So if we find your mother or your father or a sibling, we will know. Right now," he continued, "we have someone looking through old missing children reports, trying to make a connection."

"You guys still think I am just a kid, don't you." She shook her head in disgust as she spoke.

Sticking to the plan, he tried to sound convincing, "Well, the doctor who examined you said you are no more than 15, and he can prove it. I am not sure how, but since he is the doctor, I think he would know." He smiled, "Besides, it won't matter anyway when we find your family. And if we don't, it will work out."

Tori sat for a moment, considering what he had said. "But you know" she eventually observed, "I spent my whole childhood alone. Literally, never saw another child in person until we left the camp in Brazil, and I was, well, developed by then and really didn't think of myself as young anymore. I still don't. I can't get that time back, Eli. I will never have something everyone else has—

those memories. That part of my life is gone... forever."

Eli found himself lost in her words. Reaching up, he brushed her hair back from her face, his tone alluring, "So, you will have to start from here. You still have your whole life ahead of you, so make it a good one. You can't fool me, Tori. I know you will do what's right." *I only hope I can do the same.* At that instant, his phone buzzed in his pocket. Grasping it and giving it a quick irritated flick, he muttered, "Yeah?"

Tori could hear a man's voice on other end, almost certain it was Warren La Buff. "You got a meeting in Godfry's office, 20 minutes."

Eli looked at his watch, "Understood." Flipping the phone shut, he sighed to her, "I gotta go." Tori's expression was blank, but she nodded her agreement, and then watched from the window as he headed into the parking lot and climbed into his car.

Short on Time

La Buff and Godfry were already into their discussion when Eli arrived. He trod into the spacious office and took a seat in the second guest chair that stood at James Godfry's desk, wondering what his partner was up to now. Godfry didn't waste any time, and stated, "So, I hear there was some trouble over at the hospital a few days ago. Why didn't you report it?"

"I have the situation in hand, sir." Eli looked stung. "No need to get alarmed."

"I hear an orderly was attacked," his

superior continued, "That doesn't sound very in hand to me."

Warren La Buff had not been visiting the girl, but he had been watching and keeping tabs on what was going on. He had also been making a point to report back anything that gave his effort to get on with prosecution merit.

"Yes sir," Eli agreed. "A misunderstanding. We are getting really close now." *Did I really just say that?*

"And I can say for sure she knows details about the activities of the group. She says she has been with them her entire life, which means; however, they acquired her; she was very young when the event took place. I just need more time to get what we need." La Buff released a snort of contempt.

"Why do you hate her so much?" Eli turned to his partner in disgust. "You know, she wants to do the right thing. She didn't like being with those guys, and whatever part she played in their activities was under duress. She didn't want it; she didn't enjoy it. She survived, and you want to punish her for that."

"She murdered those men. She said so herself. No matter what they did, she had no right to do what she did to them." Warren La Buff's tone was matter-of-fact. "She deserves to be punished for that. God knows what else she has done we don't know about yet."

Eli stared for a moment, sadly recalling Tori's description of taking her place within the group, then replied in a lower tone as he bit out his reply, "It is far more complicated than that. Besides, you are missing the bigger picture here. Those men are already dead, and there are more of them out there still running around hurting people. She can help us get to them, but we have to earn her trust."

La Buff sneered at him, "Yeah, I saw how cozy the two of you were getting the other night on her bed. I bet she trusts you pretty good right about now."

Eli's jaw dropped as his mind raced back to the first night he had sat on the bed with her, in her room, to listen to her describe her introduction to the group. His partner must have been outside the tiny window peering in. "So, resorted to spying on a fellow agent did you? Well, I assure you, I have been completely professional with the girl, and in time I will find out everything we need to know."

"You have two days." Godfry cut in, "After that we are pulling her in and lowering the boom so to speak. We do not have time to drag this out any further." Eli nodded his understanding and stood to leave.

"Good luck with that." La Buff called after him as he headed into the hall.

Realizing he was now short on time, Eli decided to return to the hospital, *see what else I can find out tonight.* During the drive, he mentally went over the details Tori had given him so far so that it was fresh on his mind when they resumed.

When he arrived, she was not in her room, nor was she in the cafeteria. Heading out into the garden, he found her sitting on her bench, stretched out in a leisurely pose with her left leg pulled up onto the bench while leaning back, her hands behind her.

She was gazing up into the trees with the evening sun on her face. Stopping, he watched, thinking how carefree she looked as she swung her dangling right leg. He almost hated to disturb her, to make her go back to that dark place she had been telling him about on such a fine evening. After several minutes, he could wait no longer, so he stepped closer and cleared his throat.

Tori immediately sat up, dropping her propped leg and twisting to see who was there. Her heart skipped a beat when she saw him standing behind her, as she was just thinking about him and his offer of a place if she ever needed one. Standing, she glided over to meet him, resisting the urge to throw her arms around him in welcome. He was trying to keep things professional, but he was making it very hard for her to want to. "I wasn't expecting you to return tonight," she managed to keep a straight face.

Looking away, he hated lying to her, but the truth wasn't an option. He decided on something in the middle, partly true and only partly a lie, "I wanted to hear more and my calendar is empty this evening."

Tori gave a simple nod, and waved her hand for him to follow. When they arrived in her room, she wished he were there for more personal reasons, but she refused to believe that could be the case, *I'm too smart to fall for that.*

Eli sat in his chair, and Tori stretched out on the bed with her head at the foot end, not really feeling like talking. At first she lay on her stomach, half hanging off the bed so her fingers could brush the floor. *Another whimsical pose*, Eli observed, and then asked, "Are you ok? You seem a little preoccupied tonight." Looking up, Tori smiled the faintest of grins, and Eli's heart went mad inside his chest.

Rolling onto her side, he could see the curve of her breast, and a dark patch of skin that disappeared into her cleavage. *What on earth is that?* He thought he might have spoken the words aloud when her smile faded, and he realized his expression had changed.

"Forgive me." He held up an apologetic hand, "I just noticed the mark on your," *oh hell*, "breast."

Tori frowned as she peered down her shirt and realized he had seen the bite mark, probably for the first time. After a moment to compose herself, she decided that was a good place to start for the evening's tale.

"Yeah, it's from where Eddie bit me that night after Henry and I were together. He wanted to mark his turf, so I guess it is really more like a brand." Grabbing the neck of her shirt, she was able to pull it down just enough to expose the odd shaped scar. "You know, I had sex with lots of men, but Henry was the only one who ever touched me without Eddie's permission. I was his most prized possession."

"You are not a piece of property," Eli insisted, almost angrily. "I hope one day you will understand how special you truly are." His tone surprised her, and Tori felt touched that he thought so much of her.

"You have a girlfriend, or a wife, Eli?" she asked innocently enough.

"Uh, no." He shifted his gaze nervously as she recovered herself. "My job isn't really conducive to personal relationships at this point in my career. I have been pretty dedicated to my cases since my partner died three years ago. He was my mentor, and losing him like I did . . . Well, it just did something to me I can't really explain. I have just been obsessed I guess, to the point of distraction. I probably shouldn't have told you that. You have more than enough to worry about." At that moment, Eli felt genuinely guilty about the situation he seemed to be sinking deeper into by the minute.

"No, it's ok," Tori reassured him with another small grin, "It's nice to think I am not the only one who has lost things, or people, in my life. I mean, that's kinda what those fools in the group meetings talk about, but they have no idea what real pain is. If you don't mind, I would love to hear about this partner of yours. Reverse roles for the night."

Eli started to object, thinking about how little time they had left for him to find out what he needed from her. But then on second thought, it might really help her to open up to him if he were able to share this with her. He would have to be careful though, not wanting to tip her off about Castleford or his true motives for being there with her. Smiling, he agreed he could share a little, he guessed.

"Bradley Wells had been an Agent ten years when I came on board, so he showed me the ropes. They had been building a case against some really bad guys, who ran drugs and guns that we could prove, and we were getting close to making a move, when things got really crazy, and Brad was afraid we were going to lose our hold on them. So, he went in under cover while I worked from the outside trying to help him. We had been trying to get him in deeper, when I lost contact with him. Three weeks later, his body was found in a hotel, which was three years ago." Eli felt pretty safe with that version, and hoped it would do the trick.

"In a Holiday Inn," Tori replied, and without thinking, Eli agreed it was, in fact, a Holiday Inn.

Tori's face went stone cold, and she suddenly jumped up from the bed. Stepping over to the corner she had moved into the other night when they had had their confrontation, she placed her palms flat against the walls and rest the crown of her head into the crack, a form of surrender.

Immediately, Eli was alert something was wrong, and quickly joined her, trying to encourage her to tell him what was going on. Tori wouldn't answer; she stared down at her feet, mumbling to herself for several minutes. Eli stood waiting, not about to walk out on her this time.

Eventually, Tori began to shake her head side to side, and he could hear her low voice, "I'm so sorry Eli. I didn't mean it. I swear to god I didn't mean it."

Daring to touch her, he lightly stroked the back of her head and neck to comfort her, and she lifted her face and turned to look him in the eye. Tears streaked down her cheeks, her nose bright red as she cried her first real tears in years.

Eli was crushed at the sight of her, and he pulled her to him, wrapping her in his arms tightly without a second thought. Standing there, she cried hard, her body shaken by her sobs. She cried for Eli and for his friend that was taken from him. She cried for Henry, who had been good to her and paid the price. She cried for all the people who had been hurt because she had not been strong enough to stand up to Eddie the rest of his gang.

Holding her, Eli realized she knew whom he was talking about. Somewhere their paths had crossed, and she knew how he had died. A sickening thought occurred to him, and he realized up to this point he had not really believed she had killed the Dragons in that farmhouse, but it was beginning to look as if it were true after all.

Stepping back a little, Tori stared down at the floor again, her breath spastic as she tried to quell her flowing tears. Eventually looking him in the eyes, "Do you hate me?"

"No," his response was instant. "But if Eddie weren't already dead, I think I would kill him for you. Now, I need you to tell me what happened to Brad. Tell me everything."

Passing the Test

Taking a deep breath, Tori knew once she shared this part with him, there was no going back. She explained to him that the men who had ultimately ordered Brad's death were indeed very bad, and if she told him what he wanted to know, she would never live in that extra bedroom of his.

When he asked what that had to do with anything, she explained that once she had betrayed The Organization, her life would be worthless and anyone who was close to her or that she cared about would be in danger. The Organization would use such people to get to her, to hurt her, or even just because they could. Her words gave Eli a heavy ache in the pit of his stomach, and he hoped that she was wrong.

Tori began by explaining what The Organization actually was, and how the Dragons fit into it. To illustrate, she took a piece of paper and drew a simple flower in the center, like a daisy with a small round center and overly large petals.

"This," she began calmly, "is The Organization. In the center, you have a command group, which controls what everyone else is doing. It is the most secret part; the hardest part to attack or kill. Around it is the petals. These are the guys who work for The Organization, doing as the center instructs them. The flower has a purpose, like a company, that makes a product, such as drugs, that it produces and sells."

"There are insects that come and try to attack the flower," Tori drew small bugs around the illustration, "such as the cops or feds, and they are like grasshoppers eating at the flower and trying to stop it. When that happens, sometimes petals are sacrificed so that the rest of the flower can escape and survive, and like a starfish will regrow a limb, the petal will be regrown if it is lost. But sometimes, the flower gets help from the outside."

She drew a spider and a scorpion next to the flower. "Those on the outside are the ones who work around The Organization, because in the end, there are lots of flowers in the world, and they all need protecting. The ones outside The Organization are larger insects, predators like the Dragons or scorpions, or spiders. When the flower thinks it is being attacked, it calls these predators to come and defend it and take the intruder away to destroy it away from operation."

"That is what happened to Brad. When The Organization suspected him as a fed, they contacted Eddie, who picked him up, and he rode with us for a couple of weeks. Eddie told me this guy was trouble, and that we were going to eliminate him. He told me that he was a fed and must be dealt with."

Tori's lip began to quiver as she spoke. "In those couple of weeks, I thought about warning Brad about what was coming and telling him I wanted to be rescued from the Dragons, but I didn't. I just waited to see what was going to happen."

"When we arrived at the Holiday Inn, we took three rooms, Eddie and Red each took a room and Brad took one that was separated from them. This was my test, and if I passed I would earn my mark." To explain, Tori raised her sleeve above her right shoulder to expose the small black dragon tattoo that was on the back side. All full members of the group had a similar marking to identify them. Earning a mark was sacred.

"Eddie had been training me since we left the bush camp, often by taking people to use for that purpose. We left a trail of bodies from Columbia, through Panama, and up into Texas. He taught me to hunt men like they were animals, and Brad would be my first solo kill. If the hunt were successful, I would earn the mark. If it were not, I would be punished, and the training would continue."

"I went with Brad to his room. He did not know our true purpose, and accepted that we were part of The Organization. He thought he was getting closer to the center of the flower, not realizing he was being led away from it instead. He took me just as he had seen Eddie and the others do, thinking Eddie had given him a night with me as a prize for something he had accomplished within the group. He gave me a scar with a cigarette, here inside my left leg." Tori indicated where the scar lay beneath the cloth of her hospital wardrobe.

"Afterwards, I lay on the bed with him. I was naked, and I thought about whispering to him in the dark, telling him to run, to get help, or to get away. In the end, I let him fall asleep, and then I used my knife to do my secret job, the one no one but the Dragons knew was mine. Afterwards, I left him lying there, his blood soaking into the sheets and I washed myself in his shower. Then I got dressed, and I headed back to the Dragons, who would be waiting for me in their rooms."

Her face grew stony as she finished, "When I left the room, David and Chris were watching outside, and had been monitoring the room. If I had let your friend go, they would have caught him and killed him, and I would have been punished. They checked the room to be sure the job was done, and we left, headed out of town that same night. I was allowed to get my mark a few days later. Afterwards, I was given targets regularly, and I never missed. If Eddie gave the word, I put you in the ground."

"You always killed people under orders?" Eli now asked, trying to remain calm.

"I killed the dragons because I wanted to. It was time for them to die. Before that, I never did anything without orders." Tori raised her right hand to her left breast and touched her scar out of habit.

Eli wondered how long she would continue to do that, as she clearly had not even realized she had made the move or that others would notice the action. Smoothing his dark hair with his hand, he considered what he should say next.

The pause grew long, and Tori finally asked if he would like to hear about the night the Dragons got theirs, and he reluctantly agreed. She excused herself to the bathroom to wash her face and organize her thoughts before she continued.

When she returned, Eli was sitting in his chair, his face in his hands as he tried to wrap his head around what he had just heard. He had wanted to find Brad's killer ever since his body was found, and now that he knew his friend and partner had died at Tori's hand, he was heartbroken.

Sensing Eli's anguish, Tori knelt on the floor in front of him, placing her hands on his knees and gazing at him from underneath. Eli removed his hands from his face and stared down at her large innocent eyes.

Tori was such an odd combination of light and dark, having seen and experienced the worst in men, yet not knowing about the simplest parts of life most of us take for granted. Reaching out, he rested his hand on her cheek, tracing the lower line of her scar with his thumb.

Finally, he inhaled loudly, "Tell me about this, instead. You said Eddie gave it to you to keep people away. What did you mean by that?" Laying her hand on his, she thought for a moment, and then began to explain about the strange man who had caused her to earn the gruesome lines that marred the left side of her face.

"It was sometime between leaving the bush and earning my mark. Henry had been working to regain his position, and when Eddie said he had a special job that would need a man long term from outside our group, Henry told him he had just the man for the job. He contacted a guy by the name of Michael Anderson, who met up with us and rode with us for a couple of days…"

Tori suspected that Henry and Michael were somehow related, because they looked very much alike. They each had the same sandy brown hair and deep brown eyes. Coming into the group as a visitor, he watched her, but did not partake of her, and she sensed his distaste at her carousing with the crew, as if his sullen mahogany eyes were judging her in disdain.

Even though she suspected he did not approve of her, she felt him watching her often, and this made her uncomfortable. Eddie would be jealous if she showed interest in other men and that would mean trouble. Therefore, she did her best to avoid him.

After a few days, the group made a stop at a small motel, and Eddie offered Tori to Henry's friend for the night, telling him to enjoy himself, however, he liked. Now she would find out what kind of man he really was, as she had become mildly curious about the tall, dark stranger.

Unfortunately, Red insisted he needed some first, and then Michael could have what was left. Inwardly, Tori groaned at the news, as Red liked to torture her while he fucked her by hitting, pinching, and pulling her hair. Many of the scars she carried were from Red, so Tori downed a fifth of Smirnoff Silver before they went to the room. She had found that a good drink always helped her do what she had to do, as saying yes hurt far less than saying no.

The three of them entered the room, Michael leading the way. Tori followed him, with Red bringing up the rear. As soon as he shut the door,

Red punched her in the back, knocking her to the floor. Michael seemed taken completely off guard, and appearing to be a true gentleman, reached to help her, obviously disturbed.

Tori quickly gripped his arm, and as they stood, she looked him in the eye. Pushing him back, she guided him towards an overstuffed chair that sat in the corner of the room. *He can't interfere*; her mind raced. *Red won't stand for that.*

Shushing him, she told him to sit quiet and watch, but not to say or do anything, or there would be trouble. Leaning over him, she gave him a light kiss on his lips as she stroked the nape of his neck and ran her fingers through his hair. He smelled nice, and she had wished Red had let them be alone together, memories of her one night with Henry briefly flashing through her mind.

Not one for waiting, the groups second lurched forward, clenching a hand full of her hair and pulling her back towards the bed. He released her, and then slipped his hands around her waist from behind. His hands followed her front up to her breasts, cupping them gingerly for a moment, and then squeezing them so tightly that she winced in pain.

Michael folded his hands in front of his face, interlocking the digits, and allowed his index fingers to tap anxiously on his lips. Tori began to rub Red's hands to relax him and ease his strangle hold on her bruised chest. He slipped them back down to her waist, and she twisted free. It was show time, and she needed to get into the groove of the role she must now play.

Tori began to remove her clothing, kicking off her boots and sailing them towards the dresser next to her pack, while unbuttoning her pants. She pulled and lowered them, wiggling her rear end to work them down, and Red stepped back to watch. When she pulled her shirt over her head, she drew her hair through it and tossed it around in an exaggerated motion. Bent over as she unhooked her bra, she slid the straps down her arms and threw it onto the growing pile of garments.

Red sidled back towards her, this time standing in front so he could grasp her rear end and pull her body hard against his. Licking and nipping at her face and neck, he slipped his hands down into her panties and began to stroke the crack of her rear, continuing to push against her until he was fully aroused. He stepped back and grasped the button on his pants; pulling them open and unzipping them with one hand, then pushed them down just a bit. Reaching into his pants, he grasped his manhood and lifted it out, stroking it roughly with his left hand.

Tori immediately dropped to her knees, grasping it for him and licking the underside from base to tip several times. Then she took the head of it into her mouth and began working it in deeper until it was sliding down her throat. Grasping his hips, she worked him in and out for several minutes before sliding him back out of her mouth. While she worked, Red began to roll his eyes and moan deeply, pushing on the top of her head and hanging onto her hair.

Tori had learned how to please each of the Dragons, and she could anticipate what they wanted or were going to do quite easily. When he had had enough, he pulled back on her mane to remove her mouth from his throbbing organ, and she grabbed the sides of his jeans and pulled them down for him and helped him step out of them. Once he was free, he released her and she was able to stand and remove her panties before climbing onto the bed, bending over onto all fours.

Sticking her rear out and leaning on her elbows, she gripped the flower printed bedspread with her fists. Red used a small tube to grease the way with his fingers for several seconds, then pulling himself up behind her he forced his way in. She managed to keep the look of pain from her face, and she took him in silent submission. He worked her back and forth until he had penetrated her fully, slapping her on her thigh and butt cheeks every so often and grinning at the redness it produced.

The liquor was hitting her pretty good, and Tori licked her lips often, enjoying the tingle. She began to relax into the motion of his body as he pushed against her, so he grabbed her hair again, using it to gain some leverage as he worked. She was grateful for the gel that he used, as it made it hurt less, and she remembered to through in some noises that Red would find appealing while he fucked her.

Red was well built as a man, he and Eddie being the largest of the group, and she wished he did not insist that she take it all. She had complained about it once, but only once, and then learned to endure it in silence. Keeping her grasp firm, she focused on what she was doing intently.

Close to finishing, he began to push harder and faster, causing her to lose her grip and slide forward a bit, which he corrected by pulling back harder on her head for a moment, then he pushed her on forward and changed his angle of entry enough to finish the job.

He could see a small amount of blood on him when he withdrew, grinning at it with a small amount of pride. She could feel his deposit trickle out of her as she lay still and waited for Michael to begin his turn, but he did not move from the chair, sitting and watching her calmly.

Red cleaned himself and redressed, telling Michael to get it while it was fresh. Laughing, he closed the door loudly as he departed, which caused Tori to give a startled jump a full second after the door was closed.

She was growing tired, the vodka coursing through her veins, and she now deep in her stupor. She opened her eyes to look at the stranger again, who was still calmly glaring at her. She wondered what the hell he was waiting for, not that she minded sleeping through it if he didn't mind that she did. He was still sitting there when she lost consciousness, and was gone when she awoke the next morning.

What's Mine Is Mine

To her relief, Tori was alone when she woke the next morning. Her rear end ached, and she could feel the thick, sticky ooze that had been left there the night before. Moving slowly, she pulled the blankets off of herself, and fumbled her way into the bathroom, barely making it to the toilet before she spewed what was left of dinner and a fifth. Crouching on the floor next to it, she leaned against the cabinet, the cool wood refreshing to her warm cheek. After several minutes, she was able to stand and climbed into the shower on shaky limbs.

The warm water ran over her trembling body, and Tori pressed herself against the tile wall in an effort to remain standing. Turning flat against it, she was able to wash her posterior gently with soap, and then allowed the water to run across it for several minutes. Finally, she turned and washed the rest of her bruised and aching anatomy. She wondered what Michael had done to her after she passed out, but could not see any fresh wounds she could account to him.

She had known few men who weren't into kinky, and as her soft hollow between her folds of skin did not feel like it had been touched, he must have gone in the back door, the same as Red had. Standing in the warm cascade a few minutes longer, she longed for peace and freedom from her life. She would have killed herself by now, but she was too stubborn to give up. She felt like crying, but tears were for the weak. *Be strong*, she told herself; *you can do this.*

Shutting off the water, Tori stepped out into the room to dry herself and dress. She was able to put on her clean clothes from her backpack and shoved the dirty ones in a trash bag from the litter can before stuffing them into her pack to wash. She had to hurry though, so they would be dry before the Dragons were ready to roll.

Slipping into her boots and throwing on her jacket, she grabbed the bag and headed down the hall for the laundry room. Fortunately, Eddie had wanted to spend some time visiting with Michael that morning, and so she was able to finish in plenty of time before they were ready to leave.

Tori met the group out on the parking lot. Most were checking their bikes and preparing to ride. Catching her as she arrived, Eddie pulled her to him, kissing her thoroughly while squeezing her butt cheeks and massaging her aching posterior. "My god you are so hot," he breathed. "I could fuck you right here in front of god and everyone."

Tori went along, sliding her arm around him to pull him tighter against her and cooed, "After dark, Love."

Eddie laughed, thrilled, by the way, she played him, knowing it was just a game. She was good at it though, right fine bitch and the sweetest whore he had ever owned. He slapped her on her backside as he called out, "Mount up; we hit

Denver by dark." With that, everyone climbed onto their bikes, and they headed out.

Tori sat behind Eddie, as usual, and looked around for Michael, but realized he was gone. He must have been sent off on his little errand, or maybe he was dead. Either way, she was fairly certain she would never see him again. It was a long ride, and she could not stop her mind from returning to the stranger who looked so much like the man she had grown so fond of when she was young, wondering what had actually become of him.

That night, the group stopped at a rest area just outside of Denver. Curiosity got the better of her, and she asked in passing what became of him as they were unpacking their gear. Eddie didn't like her taking an interest in another man when she wasn't sucking his dick. Stopping to look at her, Tori met his gaze, a wave of fear rushing over her. She knew she was about to be punished as he stepped towards her and slapped her across her right cheek with the back of his right hand, knocking her to the ground and kicking her in the gut. Tori curled into a ball, knowing better than to fight back when he was angry.

Eddie seemed to have decided he needed to make sure she and everyone else knew whom she belonged to, and he pulled out his knife and put his knee on her chest, Red dropping down to hold her arms. He cut several deep marks into her face, above and below her left eye. The others watched from a short distance as they were accustomed to Eddie's punishments of her by now, and knew what was coming next.

The night ended the same as the first night the group had raped her, as she was then stripped and bent over the concrete table. All eleven of them had a turn, while Henry watched in obvious misery.

The next day, Eddie was so pleased with her new face, he snapped a Polaroid to record the occasion. Laughing at her, he grabbed her jaw in his right hand, and clenching it tightly pulled her face up next to his to hiss, "What's mine is mine, and *you* are mine—don't you ever fucking forget it!" He pushed her back away from him so hard that she stumbled, then fell to the ground, cutting her forearms on the rocky soil as she tried to break the fall.

*   *   *

Tori stopped at that point, having reached the part she had intended to tell, which was how she got the large scar that covered her eye. Eli sat motionless, a good listener who did not mind if she rambled at times. Tori stared at him for a minute, and then asked timidly, "Why are you here?" Eli jumped slightly, a startled expression crossing his face. "I mean, I am sure you don't come to visit me out of the goodness of your heart. You want something from me. What is it you are looking for?"

Eli felt defeated beneath the pressure of the deadline he had been given, and knew this could be his last chance to finally get what they needed. "You already gave me part of it," he admitted quietly, "But we need details. We need to know about the Dragons. Where they went, what they did, and who they did it for. What were they into exactly?"

Tori shook her head slightly; a little sad she had been right about his visits. Deep down, she would have liked that he came to her because he cared. But no one cared for her, not since Henry died. "They were into whatever was paying. As far as details, why should I give you those things? What I have already told you could cost me my life—why should I give you anymore?"

"Because it is the right thing to do," Eli said flatly. "And because you will get your freedom. You tell us everything you know, good or bad, your fault, Eddie's fault, whatever it is, and you get your new life. I know you suffered and did not choose the life you had, but this is your chance to walk away clean, start fresh. You can be anyone you want to be." His voice held promise, and he spread his hands as if to offer her the world. "It's like going to church to visit the priest. All you have to do is confess everything, and all will be forgiven."

Tori eyed him warily, not really believing him, but not really having a choice either. She was used to doing what she had to do, and not seeing another way out, she agreed, "But I want it in writing," she stipulated.

"You can have it in writing," he promised.

Having abruptly come to an agreement, Eli realized they had to work quickly, and pulled out his phone to make a call. It was after ten, but with the two days deadline, there was no time to waste. Reaching Debra Paisley, he explained to her what was going on in a hurried manner, and then asked if she could meet with him at the office in the morning. He knew he might catch some flack over his actions in the end, but he wanted Tori to walk into the federal office looking and feeling her best. He knew Debra would know what to do to help her. He left her with a quick peck on the cheek and headed off to plan their next move.

*   *   *

When Eli Founder entered Tori's room the next morning, she was stretched between the chairs next to the window, enjoying a book and the morning sun. She looked up as he came in, but no smile of greeting crossed her lips. One might have taken that to mean she was displeased to have him there, but it was actually quite the opposite, as she was practiced at hiding behind her placid expressions.

Tori had grown quite fond of Eli, and in the last few days had begun thinking that he could actually be considered a friend. Closing the book, she pulled her feet out of the other chair so that he could sit down and share what surely must be good news from his excited smile.

"How are you feeling?" Eli asked breathlessly. A small nod was her positive response as he adjusted himself into the chair more comfortably. "Well, talkative as ever." He laughed at his own joke, and then continued. "I was able to meet with Debra this morning. She is going to help us put our plan in motion." She raised an eyebrow at him, not sure exactly what 'our plan' even was. Realizing he was getting ahead of himself, he corrected, "Let's go have breakfast, and I will explain everything."

They moved in unison through the halls towards the cafeteria, and Eli began to outline what he and Debra had lined out. Agent Paisley was going to bring a surprise for Tori—a way to cover her scar so that no one would even know it was there when they saw it. "Then she will take you shopping," Eli explained. "That way you can choose clothes you will be comfortable in when I take you to meet the committee." Apprehension quickly shot through her, and Tori felt very nervous about her choice to help him.

"And what exactly is it they want to know? I mean, I really don't want to share everything with them that I have been telling you or the doctor." Tori felt very vulnerable at the idea of describing how she was abused to a room full of strangers.

In response, Eli shifted nervously realizing she might not be happy when she found out what he had done. "You won't have to share those things," he admitted his guilt in a submissive tone, "I have typed up your 'story' and submitted it with my report thus far. They already know what happened to you. What they need to hear from you is details on The Organization, the Dragons, and basically where the bodies are buried."

Tori kept walking, eyes straight ahead, and

replied, "Well then, we are gonna need a map." Eli gave her a sideways glance, and wondered if she had just made a joke.

They ate in relatively comfortable silence, Tori stealing glances at him and thinking about what was coming. She wanted Eli to be her friend. She needed to know he was on her side, not just doing his job.

Once they had eaten, Eli walked Tori back to her room, where a large brown paper bag was waiting on her bed. She eyed the bag suspiciously, so Eli waved a hand towards it and told her to open it with a mysterious grin, as it was for her. Peering down into the dark sack, she couldn't tell what was inside, so she turned the bag upside down to dump the contents onto her bed.

It was clothes—a plain white tee shirt, jeans and sneakers. Eli stepped into the hall and closed the door so she could change. When she joined him outside, he led her down the passage and out to the parking lot, where his car was waiting.

Climbing inside the front seat, she looked

back at the hospital and wondered if she were ever coming back. "They don't care if you take me out like this?" she asked vacantly.

"Not really," Eli replied, "You have more or less been in federal custody the whole time, so no, they really didn't care if I take you out," *which is mostly true,* he rationalized.

They arrived at his apartment a short time later and climbed into the elevator. Eli explained about the two day deadline and that they only had one day to effectively prepare for her appearance before the committee.

When they stepped through his front door, Debra was already there waiting, along with a case full of supplies. Eli introduced them to one another, and then excused himself as he needed to head into the office to do some paperwork. "I will meet you back here this evening," he told Tori with a smile and a quick embrace.

Out on the Town

Debra had Tori sit in a chair in the kitchen and walked around so that she could look her over as she gave her the run down on what they were going to be doing to prepare. "I have some good things for you," she stated, trying to sound upbeat. However, she suspected from her posture that the girl was not in the mood to be social or hear any kind of news, good or bad. Debra stood in front her, and moved her hand to lift Tori's chin and have a look at her face more closely. Tori swung in reaction, knocking her hand away and glared up at her intently.

"I don't like to be touched," she stated angrily. Then, blinking a few times, she continued, "You may be the first woman to ever speak to me that wasn't a cashier or a waitress." Debra grabbed another chair and pulled it over directly facing her charge so she could look her in the eye and sat down.

Tori gave an exaggerated sigh, and sat staring at the older woman. *What is the point in resisting?* At that moment, she longed for a bottle of Denaka, wanting nothing more than to be left alone. She was doing what Eli wanted her to do, but she didn't feel at all good about it.

"Well," Debra began, "We have to get you ready for your big day. You want to face the committee with confidence, show them you are a mature young lady who can handle herself." Her smile was small but genuine. "So let's set some goals, ok?"

She waited for Tori to give her a signal she understood, but the other woman sat motionless, not making a sound. Taking the silence to be a form of agreement, she continued. "First off, I have found something to help you feel more comfortable when dealing with people. It is a special makeup that will cover your scar. No one will know it is there, unless you tell them or show them. We want to improve your self-confidence, and this will help."

"I don't wear makeup," Tori's tone was flat. The truth was, she had never had any to put on or try, even if she had wanted to. "I don't really know anything about 'girl stuff' like that."

"That's ok," Debra felt her heart warm a bit, suspecting this was why Eli had become so attached to the simple way the girl spoke.

The group had met a few times over the course of her internment to share details about their portion of the job at hand, and he had warned them that Tori's past was heartbreaking, but her spirit was solid like a rock. Debra was very glad she was going to be a part of setting her off on this journey, one that would change everything for her and give her a future to look forward to.

Over the next two hours, Debra showed Tori

how to use the makeup she brought and made small talk, trying to learn more about her life from Tori's own mouth. In the end, she found that the girl said very little without purpose and decided that practicing social interaction was going to be a necessary challenge.

Finally ready, the pair set out to gather what Tori would need in the way of clothing and personal items. Exiting the building, she felt frightened, and yet unexplainably excited to be going on the first truly female activity of her life—shopping. She had never spent time in the company of another woman, and was faintly curious now about how her own gender lived from day to day.

They made their way down the local shopping strip in relative quiet. As the day progressed, Tori began to relax, allowing Debra to make suggestions about types of clothing without protest. She had always worn what she was given and could not recall ever picking out her own clothes.

Now that she had the chance, Tori

entertained the idea of choosing things that were very different from what she had worn before. She tried on many tops and pants and even a dress, which she had never worn in her life.

Debra smiled encouragingly, "See, now you can be anyone you want to be. No one will know where you came from unless you tell them, and your differences will become much smaller."

After it was all said and done; however, Tori chose clothes that were very similar to what she was familiar with: jeans, boots, long sleeved tees, and a new leather jacket that made her truly excited to be getting new clothes. *Now if I just had a bike to go riding around on, now that I am dressed for it.* Debra even let her choose jewelry and sunglasses, and was a little surprised at how old the girl really looked when she was all fixed up and back in her element. Tori appeared cool, confident, and ready for anything.

At the end of their spree, they stopped at an outdoor café for a late lunch. As they sat at the table, surrounded by shopping bags, Tori could not hold back her feelings of excitement.

Debra was smiling ear to ear at the sight of her project, "Have you felt like people were staring at you today?"

With a quick glance around, Tori realized that people actually had not been gawking at her at all, and for an instant looked as if she were going to smile. "I do like the makeup," she admitted with a small nod while looking down at her food shyly. "I haven't noticed anyone staring at me the way they have for so long. Thank you. And for the clothes," she added in a light tone, "I will enjoy them, I think."

Debra smiled broadly, shaking her head in agreement, "So, have you thought about what you would like to do when you are released?"

Tori considered the question for a moment, then asked quietly, "Do you think they are really going let me go if I tell them what they want to know? I mean, I have done a lot of pretty bad things. I can't imagine them just cutting me loose. And there is the thing Eli said about my only being 15. How do we get that taken care of? I know I am older than that, but I have no idea how to prove it."

Debra had to agree; she did not look that young at the moment. But then again, she wasn't about to cross Godfry by revealing his plan for the girl, so she remained silent.

"Other than that, I have no idea what I am going to do. I never really had to do anything for myself, as it was all more or less provided for me. I have never had a job, and I don't really know much about work that is legal. I do know about motorcycles, like how to repair them and stuff like that so I could work on those. And I love music. Henry taught me to play the guitar, but I doubt you can actually make a living at that." Running out of breath, Tori shrugged and let her shoulders drop, looking slightly depressed now. "I have no idea what I am going to do."

Debra laughed out loud. "That was the most I have heard you say yet! You're right; there are a lot of things that will have to be decided in the immediate future. But think of it this way, now you can dream about your prospects. Somewhere down the line, you may meet that special guy and have a family of your own. Who knows?" The color drained from Tori's face, and Debra stopped her train of thought, "What's the matter?"

Tori didn't reply. She sat for a moment, rubbing her lips with her fingers, thinking about what her new friend had just said. She was considering if she could share the truth with her. Finally, she decided it was worth the risk, "Do you mind if I tell you something personal?"

Debra was quick to reply, "Of course not, tell me anything you like," and sat forward in her chair so she could listen better.

Tori began by explaining how the Dragons had lived in a camp in South America until she was old enough to travel with them cross country on their motorcycles. Debra nodded and explained that she had read Eli's report and was familiar with her story up to the point of leaving the 'bush camp.' Tori wasn't sure she liked the idea of so many people being "familiar with her story," but decided to continue.

Once the group had left their camp in Brazil,

it took them six weeks to make their way into Texas. They crossed over in El Paso, and then headed east, making their way to Florida. Just before crossing from Texas into Louisiana, Eddie purchased a kit from a drug store and put it in the saddle bag on his bike for later, saying there was something he needed to check. At dusk, they stopped as usual, and Tori prepared for the nights events, as she was becoming accustomed to being the entertainment after dark.

She had been slowly learning what to do to please each of the guys, and had already come to realize that they hurt her less when she did things for them that they liked. Henry had also adjusted to their new roles, and would sleep away from the group, since he was forbidden to touch her and did not like to see her with the other men. Things had fallen into a routine of sorts, and seemed to be going better for her in a manner of speaking.

The following morning, Eddie pulled a small tube out of the box and handed it to her while she was getting dressed. Staring intently down at it, she could see a small window in the side with a pink line, and a cap on the end that covered a white stick.

Looking at Eddie in uncertainty, he growled, "Just go pee on the stick and bring it back." Tori found a place that was more private, and did as she was instructed, returning the plastic tube to him a few minutes later.

Taking it from her, he looked down at the small device, shaking his head for a moment. Calling Red over, he informed him they were going to need some supplies and a place to crash for a day or two. Word spread quickly through the small group, and although Tori wasn't sure what was going on, she could tell by everyone's mood it couldn't be good.

Red made a disgusted noise at the news, but Eddie remained calm, "No worries man, we're gonna take care of it."

When it got close to dark, the guys started looking for a house that appeared abandoned or where the family was away. Soon finding the later in a secluded area, they broke in and made themselves at home. Gathering an odd mix of items in the largest bedroom, Eddie told Tori to take a hot shower. Handing her a large bathrobe, she was to wear only that when she got out.

The girl took her time, having discovered showers since they hit the road. She had only had a few, but already regarded them as almost sacred time to herself and the chance to be clean as she never had been before. Stepping out of the stall, she dried herself and put on the bulky cover. Once she left the bathroom and saw the small gathering around the bed, she had a bad feeling about what was going to happen next.

Eddie was being very kind to her, kinder than she ever remembered him being, talking to her sweetly while leading her over to the bed. His bizarre behavior was making Tori nervous. He lifted the robe off of her leaving her standing naked in front of the small group that was hovering around the bed, which made her even more uncomfortable. She was instructed to lie down, and she complied, but felt like her heart would leap out of her chest it was beating so wildly.

Not understanding what was going on, Tori lay back, looking at the pile of towels and other odd items that had been gathered on the dresser to the right of her. Two of the guys sat next to her chest, one on each side, stretching her arms out and laying across them so that she was thoroughly pinned. Two others sat next to her hips, bending her legs at the knee, and pulling her ankles up until her heels touched her rear end. They then wrapped their arms around her legs to hold them in the awkward position.

Tori could see Eddie holding a wire hanger that had been unfolded and bent strangely, and suddenly she had to know what in the hell was going on, so she began to cry out as she panted from the uncomfortable contortion she was being held in. David, who was holding her right arm, stroked her hair and leaned closer to her face to whisper, "Just relax, baby girl."

Tori stopped struggling as she stared into David's green eyes. "Tell me what's going on," her tone pleading.

"It doesn't matter," he replied, "It has to be

done."

She could feel fingers touching her and the coldness of the gel they used on her rear, but they were putting it into her other folds of flesh and hollow. *Is that the metal hanger I can feel down there?*

"Don't move," David warned her. "Just lie still and focus on me." He continued to stroke her hair, scooting down so he was still holding her, but could nuzzle her face with his nose. She could feel his breath on her skin and for a moment, she was able to relax just a bit.

Suddenly, a sharp stabbing pain shot up inside her, and Tori screamed out in agony. "We should have let her have a drink for the pain," someone said. "She can't," was the reply, "we don't want her to bleed to death." The voices were jumbled, several of the guys talking at once.

The pain continued to spike and subside for several minutes, David doing his best to console her. Tori began to try to fight them, but there was no way she could push them off from the way they held her. After what seemed like an eternity, she could feel warm fluid dripping out of her aching orifice, like her menstrual blood, only heavier.

Then she could see Eddies' shoulder moving as he was stabbing her insides with the crooked end of the hanger. "Are you sure it will work?" a deeper voice asked.

"Yeah, it will work," Eddie replied, "Just have to scar it up pretty good or it will just happen again."

When he was finished, she was released, and they pulled her up to the end of the bed and onto the floor, where they had her kneel over a large porcelain bowl they had found in one of the rooms. Tori hovered on all fours, with her hips lowered over the wide opening like she was going to pee in it, and she could feel the blood running out of her and dripping into the vessel.

Several times, larger chunks of thick mucus feeling material also passed, and she could feel small streams of liquid running down her legs. As she watched the container, she began to sob as she realized what they had done to her. Laying the robe over her back, someone darkened the bowl so she could not see what she was passing, but it was too late, and the damage was done.

After about half an hour, the bowl was removed, and she was lifted back onto the bed. She felt faint but remained conscious throughout the inspection of her injured female anatomy. She didn't try to struggle and lay still even when Eddie pressed on her stomach, causing horrific waves of pain as her freshly mutilated uterus contracted.

David lay with her, a small lamp for light, while the rest of the crew spread out into the other rooms of the house to get some sleep. Spooned up behind as she lay on her right side, he stroked her gently, whispering to her soothingly, but Tori gave no response. Her innards ached and throbbed throughout the night, and her sleep was not restful.

The next morning, she was bathed with warm water and allowed to walk around, but only for a short amount at a time. While she was up, the bed was changed so she could lay in fresh blankets and towels. The Dragons had never really cared for her before, and the fact that they did so now only made her despise them more. Lying on the bed again, she could still feel the blood dripping from her, and she realized it must have been her period or something like it.

The guys were calm, so she was fairly certain she would live, and Eddie checked her several times, even taking her temperature as part of the routine. She was able to sleep some that afternoon, and in between was given light soups and broth to drink.

By the next day, she was able to move around more and took another shower to wash the blood from her legs. They wouldn't allow her to get dressed, but found a gown that belonged to a woman who lived in the house and gave it to her to wear. Tori still did not feel hungry, but they insisted that she eat. When she was left alone, she lay on her side in the bed and wept.

The old couple who lived in the house returned the third night, and the Dragons dealt with them, but their untimely arrival meant they would have to move on by the next morning. Just before daybreak, Tori was awakened and told she could dress. As soon as she was ready, they mounted up and moved on.

She was in pain while they rode, and she made loud grunts whenever they hit a bump or rough spot. She clung to Eddie tightly, fearing she would fall from the bike, and he rubbed the backs of her hands often as she clutched his broad chest. Finding a spot for the night early, she was again allowed to rest. For the next few weeks, she was shown how to satisfy a man orally instead of the usual nightly routine, but after a month things were back to normal, and no one ever spoke of the event again.

"So you see," Tori explained, "I will never have a family of my own. My life has never been, nor will it ever be, normal."

Debra stared at her for several minutes, digesting what she had just heard. Sadly, Dr. Bennet had told the committee Tori suffered from a rare uterine disorder and would probably never be able to have children. At least now she knew that part of his report was true, and she also knew why.

Live While We Can

Tori's mood was somber as they returned to Eli's apartment. He was already home and waiting for their return. Sensing her distress when they came in, he placed a hand on her hip to pull her close, then wrapped his arms around her for a firm hug.

She stood in his embrace for a full minute, clinging to him and taking comfort in his caring gesture. Debra finally cleared her throat to break them up, and Eli smiled sheepishly as Tori stepped away from him. "May I take a shower," she asked softly, "Or am I going back to the hospital?"

"No, you can shower if you want. I am going

to put you up in my spare room tonight. We will head up to my office tomorrow to introduce you properly to the committee." He smiled brightly at her, but Tori gave no response. She simply grabbed the bag that had her new sleeping garments and underclothes in it and went off to find the bathroom.

Debra waited until they heard the sound of running water before she grabbed his arm, "Oh, my god, what they did to her was horrible!"

"What did she say?" he asked cautiously. Eli was surprised Tori was able to talk to Debra so freely, as he had been concerned all day about her reaction to spending time with a fellow female, maybe for the first time in her life.

"Well, remember what Dr. Bennet said about Asherman's Syndrome? They gave her an abortion with a clothes hanger and scarred her on purpose to prevent her from getting pregnant again. He estimated it happened three years ago, but wasn't for sure. She said it took place about six weeks after they left the bush camp. Jesus, Eli, I don't see how she is ever going to have a normal life after all she has been through!" Debra lamented while shaking her head.

"We will take care of her, Deb." Eli assured her. "She is strong. She will find her way."

The two of them were still talking quietly when they heard the water cut off in the bathroom. Debra decided she wanted to be gone before she came out, so hastily said good night and made for the door. Tori exited with a puff of steam just as the apartment exit closed behind her, and Eli turned to show Tori to her room.

Again, he smiled warmly and tried to be positive in light of what he had just heard. Tori looked desolate as he led the way to the smaller bedroom across the hall from his own. He had placed her bags on the chair beside the door so she would be able to dress in her new clothes for the meeting tomorrow.

Turning, he noticed her bare legs were clean shaven and silky smooth in the pair of boxers she wore to sleep in. His eye's climbing slowly, and he liked the way the tee shirt fit the curve of her waist and more snuggly around her chest. For a moment, he paused and thought about her bare breasts beneath it.

When his eyes made it to her face, he could see she had watched him as he looked her up, and she asked curtly, "Like what you see?"

He had been caught, and his face turned a bright shade of red. "I am so sorry," he stammered." I did not mean to make you uncomfortable," and began backing out the door.

Turning quickly, Eli darted to the kitchen to check on the small dinner he had put into the oven for them and made some fresh tea. Tori sat on the bed, thinking she might just go to sleep without eating, but her rumbling belly convinced her otherwise. She thought about slipping on her pants before she went down the hall, then thought better of it and headed to the kitchen to find out what smelled so good.

When she entered the room, Eli shot her a quick glance, then put his eyes back on his work to avoid a second incident in one evening. Stopped in the doorway, she noticed the table was set, and everything seemed to be in perfect order. She thought about how Debra had put her makeup on while she sat in one of the chairs just that morning, but it seemed long ago now. Tori had washed it away while in the shower and was now her normal self.

Looking over towards Eli, she could see he was busily putting the finishing touches on their meal, and she tried to fill the awkward silence, "You need any help?"

"No, No, I got it," he replied. "Just pour yourself some tea and have a seat. This is almost ready."

Tori placed ice in a glass and poured the fresh brewed beverage, then as she placed it on the table, decided to make a glass for him, as well. Working together, they moved the items to the table, and Tori stopped abruptly as she realized something was different about him. Grabbing his arm, she pulled him up in front of her, and they stood face to face, Tori now looking cleanly over the top of his head. "You got shorter!" she exclaimed.

"I'm not . . . wearing my shoes." Eli stammered. "We all have things about us we would like to change. I would like to be taller. Not that I am short, I'm just . . . not tall." He tried to smile, but she could tell he was still self-conscious about what had happened a few minutes prior, and now she had pointed out a flaw about him that he did not like people to notice.

Tori felt a surge of affection towards her friend, and she gave him a small smile as she whispered in a sultry voice, "You're tall enough. I'm the one who is out of proportion, amazon woman I am." Standing at least six foot with no shoes, Tori was clearly taller than him, and privately wished she were not.

Eli had to laugh at their awkwardness together. They had spent weeks in each other's company, but now they were in new territory. Holding on to his smile, their mood was noticeably lighter for the meal.

Sitting to their broiled steaks, small baked

potatoes, steamed veggies and dinner salad, Tori remembered the home cooked meals of old, when she was young, and Henry taught her about eating well. She was glad to see Eli had a good diet and chose the kinds of foods she had grown to love. They ate in virtual silence, with only the occasional comment as to the tastiness of their food. She felt comfortable with the man who sat across the table, the shadow of what loomed ahead of her in the back of her mind.

Finishing their meal, She inquired about the apartment and how long he had lived there. Eli answered her questions, an odd feeling in the pit of his stomach. He realized he had never heard her make small talk before. They had slipped back into French while dining, and he was picking up a wistful vibe from her now. She was almost smiling as they spoke, and he asked if she were ready for a tour. Reluctant to give up the comfort of the kitchen and the company, she half-heartedly agreed.

The wall between the kitchen and living room had a large open window so that the two rooms felt open, and conversation could pass between easily. To the left of the kitchen door, the living room was sparse, with a single couch and table in front of it that was bare. A massive television hung on the far wall, and she could picture Eli sitting there flipping through channels in boredom.

Back to the right, the bathroom was the first entrance on the right as you walked down the narrow hall; a small washer and dryer hidden behind shuttered doors across from it. Tori's room lay behind the next door down on the right. She stepped back inside the small square of space as he described his plans for improvements.

"Of course, if you were to decide to stay here for a time, you could decorate the room, however, you wanted. It is after all an empty slate pretty much at the moment." True enough; the room was barren except for a small twin bed with a mismatched nightstand and a single dining table chair next to the door, which did not match the kitchen furniture.

Across the hall from her bedroom stood Eli's chamber, which was a great deal more finished inside. Once they moved through the portal, Tori felt overjoyed with the deep browns and greens he had chosen for his palette and felt as if she had been whisked back to the jungles of South America.

The room was quite cozy. It held a king sized bed, comforting deep stained wood on the head and footboards. To either side stood matching nightstands and a dresser that filled the wall to the right of the door, completing the circle to the back wall of the room.

A live tree stood in the far left corner, next to a door that led to a small bathroom opposite the bed. The floors of the apartment were hardwood, but there was a large shaggy rug that covered the floor in this room that dampened the sound and made it feel as if it wrapped around a person, drawing them in tightly.

"I have never had a home," Tori breathed, "much less a bedroom such as this. It is amazing, Eli."

He was standing on her left as she hovered

next to the foot of his extravagant bed, her right hand resting on the corner post of the footboard. The room was so large, and she had a feeling this was his favorite place to be. Cutting her eyes to give him a sideways glance, she wondered how many women he brought to this room for the night; her heart pained with jealousy.

As if he had read her thoughts, he smiled broadly, "Too bad I spend every night here alone."

Tori turned her head to look at him fully, raising her left hand to meet his. She dropped her eyes to watch their fingers mingle, her heart beginning to race.

"I think it might be time for bed," Eli spoke softly. Tori breathed an agreement, but did not move to leave the room, her bare feet planted firmly in the luxury of the mat beneath them.

Her eyes skimming up his body, she noticed he was still fully clothed except for his shoes that had been removed. *I wonder if he likes to be undressed, or if he would want to do that for himself?*

Eli was not a large man, his chest and shoulders less broad than most men she had known. His light grey shirt covering them, she noted his tie had also been removed, and the top few buttons were open, which allowed a few dark brown hairs to escape and tease.

Her eyes continued to climb, pausing at his closed lips that curved into a half smile. Leaning closer to him, she moved her gaze to his blue eyes that were deeper than her own, with flecks of brown and green. He was watching her intently, and he swallowed hard as he considered what might happen next.

"You should go to your room," he instructed directly.

Tori only stared at him for several moments, then spoke in a low voice, "Eli, what were you thinking when you looked at me earlier? Do you think that I am . . . attractive?"

Curling his fingers around hers more tightly, he shifted his gaze to her lush lips and replied, "I think you're beautiful. You caught my eye while I was sitting on a hard wooden chair in a cold hospital room, and you have been taking my breath away ever since." He gave a lopsided smile as memories of her flashed through his mind, and he could see her sitting on a bench in the sun, watching the birds and swinging her leg all over again.

"I am not beautiful, Eli." Tori's voice picked up a sad tone for a moment. "You can see the scars as well as I can feel them." She rubbed the backs of his fingers with her thumb, twisting her body slightly from side to side. She had only ever been with one man because she wanted to be, and even then she was not sure she really had a choice.

Tori wanted to make love to Eli—to pour herself onto him and please him with every ounce of her being. She wanted it to be perfect for him, and she knew she wasn't perfect. Sensing her somberness, Eli shifted towards her, allowing their lips to meet. He raised his free hand to her waist and rubbed her firm skin through the thin cotton tee. Instantly, Tori was on fire, and she released the post and his hand simultaneously, each grasping at his fine clothes and working quickly to remove them.

For a moment, Eli was startled by her action, a split second of doubt as he realized her intentions. Her kiss was intoxicating, and his mind quickly became muddled as his shirt fell to the floor behind him. Her hands moved with haste to remove his belt and unlock the pants that hid his manhood before running her fingers playfully across his chest.

His hair was not so thick there, and she could easily feel the skin beneath it. The rubbing made her fingers tingle, and she continued to steal kisses from him, causing her lips to burn. Quietly, she whispered to him as her digits danced and teased. She was an expert at this, and he was quickly losing himself in her.

Grasping her hands suddenly, he pulled himself back, "I can't do this. I want to, but it isn't our time yet."

Tori's mind was clouded by desire, and she barely heard his words. Her reply was a low murmur, "Live while we can, Eli. Tomorrow is only a promise, and this is the moment that matters."

She freed her hands and put them back on his burning skin, sliding them around to his smooth back, pulling him against her trembling body. Her left hand shot up, caressing the back of his head and the nape of his neck, her grip firm with need. Raising his hand to her waist again, he could feel his resolve weakening.

Nuzzling and biting at his ear, she asked if he preferred the light or the dark, and he stepped away from her for a moment to switch off the bright overhead light. There were two small, round lights on the ceiling that shown down on his tree, and they bathed the room in a warm, soft glow. He smiled as he sidled back up to her, realizing he could never deny her.

Nothing Is Forever

Their hands began to glide across one another, removing clothes and revealing tantalizing flesh. Tori felt free, as her heart beat hard and fast with joy and excitement. Taking control of him, she pushed his naked body back onto the bed. He worked his way up, sliding on his back, lying across the bed from side to side. She loved running her fingertips over him, and used her lips to tease him in sensitive places.

He could see the shadow of her scarred left breast hanging down as she bent over him, and thought about what it had meant in the past. The scar was faded now, only a small part of her being, and she was more beautiful to him now than ever.

Her hands were strong and sure as she gripped him, her thumb massaging the tender spot where the head of him met the shaft. She licked and teased him mercilessly before taking him into her mouth and easily into her throat. He rubbed the top of her head gently as she pleased him, driving him to the edge of insanity.

When Eli began to grasp fistfuls of the comforter, his moans growing louder, he began to flex his legs beneath her; Tori raised her head to lick the tip of him playfully and smiled up at him. The look of delight on his glistening face touched her heart like sunshine.

She could feel the ooze of her own juices between her legs and her warm interior throbbed and ached, yearning to have him inside her. Slowly, she slithered up his body and allowed her belly to sink against his chest, her breast hanging over his mouth so that he could lick her nipple and twirl around it with his tongue in torment. She then slid her body back down into position above him.

Eli could not tell if she were teasing him or

herself, but her movements were driving him out of his mind. Releasing the blankets, he put his hands on her, trying if not succeeding to be gentle as he moved his fingers over her smooth skin.

He slid his right hand around her back and caressed the part of her just above where her rear split, sliding it up and down so he could feel the swell of her butt cheek and massage it playfully. He wasn't inside her yet, and his hardened organ was pulsing with anticipation of the moment.

With his left hand, Eli grasped her right breast, careful not to grasp it too firmly. He wanted the action to convey how much he treasured her, and he slid his thumb lightly across the tightened peak to flick it back and forth, listening to her pant in return.

Using his newfound handholds, he pushed her down within his reach and lifted his hips to make his way inside her. The wetness of her slippery hollow made the path easy to maneuver, and he pulled her hard on top of himself.

Tori gasped at his actions and their bodies

quickly found a synchronized movement that sent waves of pleasure through them both. She was kissing him; her hands unable to find a resting spot as they moved between toying with the almost bare skin on his chest and rummaging through his thick shocks of coal black hair that topped his head. He was thrusting inside her, and she had never known such pleasure.

Eventually, her knees grew tired. Sensing this, Eli pushed her off of the top of himself and over onto her back. Moving on top of her, he reentered her with ease, grasping her silky legs and holding them spread wide as he drove his way between.

Tori wrapped her long limbs around him, hugging him to her tightly, swells of joy and longing spewing inside her. *Nothing is forever*, she thought, *but this moment is ours.* She had never been happier listening to the fwap-fwap sound that it made when their bodies were in motion. Finally, she raised her feet, lifting them towards the ceiling as the intensity mounted, and there was a loud crescendo of yelps and moans as they reached the climax of their journey.

Panting heavily, Eli remained on top of her, the undulating waves of her soft interior tickling him as his pulsing ceased inside her, and he began to deflate. Reaching up, he stroked her hair, his sweat dripping onto her face as he moved to nuzzle her jawline and brush her bruised lips with his own. Tori was breathing deeply, holding him close to her and panting in desperate satisfaction.

She did not want the moment to end and held him in place when he tried to free her, whispering for him to wait a minute longer. Propping himself up on his left elbow, he slipped a bit to her side; he blew puffs of air on her cheek to cool her, and she smiled weakly as her palms tingled and she felt too weak to move. *My god, if only we could lie like this forever,* he thought.

Their breathing returning to normal, the pair lay with legs stretched, and Eli ran his fingers lightly up and down the full length of her torso, hugging the curves and causing her to pant loudly at his touch. He loved her smile and felt as if he had waited a lifetime to behold it. She reached with her left hand to catch his fingers again, lightly interlocking them with her own.

"Thank you," she whispered hoarsely.

Eli pulled her hand up to kiss it and said with a chuckle, "No, thank you."

The air had grown cooler around them, and they shifted to face the right direction on the bed, sliding beneath the covers to snuggle as they slept. Eli spooned himself up behind her so he could toy with her chest as he drifted off to sleep.

Soon, Tori could hear the deep inhalations as they overtook him, and she sighed in contentment, cupping his hand as it held her left breast. Looking down, she could see the scar between his fingers and found herself remembering what it meant— *I will always know my place.*

Tori had a new place now, in Eli's arms, but deep down she was afraid it would not always be so, and the thought returned to her, *nothing is forever.* She hoped that she was wrong, and they would have many more nights like this to share, but in case not, at least they had this one, and the thought pleased her as she too drifted off to sleep.

The pair arose early the next morning, each getting a shower and dressing for Tori's big day. Eli was going to take her in, a full day before his deadline, and she intended to tell the committee everything she knew about The Organization and the Dragons.

Tori dressed in the new clothes she had chosen the day before, but they were exactly what she would have worn when she was part of that terrible procession, except for the long sleeves.

She had chosen those to cover the scars on her arms, as the makeup covered the one on her face. Debra was right; Tori was now free to be whoever she chose to be, and knowing that gave her strength to hope her new life was truly coming to be.

It took Tori's novice hands much longer to put the make-up in place, but Eli watched her patiently. "We have all the time you need," he reassured her, "A whole day, in fact, if you want it."

Tori was tempted to take him up on that, and

briefly allowed herself to picture the two of them on his bed making love for hours. Shaking herself back, she continued to draw the lines around her eyes and darken her scarred brow until it was identical to the other.

Turning to ask if she had done well, Tori felt the lump in the pit of her stomach beginning to grow. It was her time to speak out for what was right and to reveal what she knew that would help bring justice for the families of everyone who had been hurt by her tormentors. *Making love will have to wait.*

When she was ready, the two of them headed down to the parking garage, where Eli's car awaited. While they stood side by side in the descending elevator, Tori unexpectedly swung around to face him, looking at his lips briefly before she kissed him forcefully, and then slipped back to her place beside him.

A sly smile formed on her lips as he looked over at her, and he hoped she would not do that in public. "Everyone still thinks you are under-aged," he reminded her, "So let's keep the displays of affection private. Besides the fact that I am a Federal Agent, and you are more or less my prisoner."

Giving him a sideways look as they exited the elevator, she tossed lightly, "I told you, I am not under-aged, but I will keep my hands, feet and lips to myself if that is what you wish."

Eli laughed at her mock bow and the wafting motion she made with her hand. The girl was truly coming to life before his very eyes, and he only hoped he would be there to see how it all worked out.

Coming Clean

Eli had Tori sit on a bench next to a door on the 6ᵗʰ floor labeled 'conference room' and stepped inside. After several minutes, the door opened and a man about Eli's height came out. When Tori stood and faced him, the man extended his hand and announced in a friendly voice, "Hi, I am Doug Seeming." Tori looked down at his hand for several seconds, but did not reach out to shake it, before meeting the man's gaze.

Tori had grown familiar with Eli and rather enjoyed the feel of his hands and skin. However, this man was a stranger, and she wanted no part of coming in contact with him, even in such a socially accepted fashion.

Realizing the awkwardness of the moment, Doug stepped aside and bade her, "Please come in," so Tori stepped through the door, pausing on the other side to take in the layout of the enormous room.

The meeting room was quite large, with a dozen or so six foot tables in various locations. On the far side, was a group of three tables arranged to form a U with a single leather covered chair sitting in the opening. The members of her committee were sitting around the tables facing the chair, two on each side and one empty chair at the bottom for Doug.

Tori noticed Debra Paisley seated on the far side, facing them as they entered, but she chose to ignore the woman in case their prior meeting was supposed to have been a secret. Next to her sat Eli, who gave her a warm half smile of approval as she stood before the group.

Doug moved into the room behind her and indicated the empty chair, "Its ok, go on and have a seat." Tori thought his smile was too large, exposing too many teeth, but moved to comply without argument.

As she arrived at the chair, Doug, could not resist the question, "how tall are you?" He was genuinely surprised, having expected a much smaller girl. Tori considered the question while she took her seat, then with an upturned palm replied she didn't really know. Warren La Buff made a rather noisy 'ugh' of disbelief at her response, and she glared at him as she recalled their previous interactions.

Coming to her rescue, Dr. Bennet spoke up on her behalf, "She is 6 feet tall." He went on to explain how he had used her bones to help estimate her age, clarifying, "We may never really know how old she is if we are unable to find her true identity and birth records. However, what we can say for fairly certain is, when she stops growing, she will be about 15 years of age." He gave Tori a warm smile of encouragement as he finished shoring up their agenda.

So this is the proponent of the erroneous age theory. I will have to have a word with him about that, she thought to herself in disgust.

"I'm not sure you remember me," James Godfry took over the conversation smoothly, "But I am Special Agent Jim Godfry. I was able to be at the hospital when you first awoke. I'm sorry I haven't made it by for another visit, but I assure you Dr. Carlisle and Agent Founder have been keeping us apprised of your progress."

Her heart pounding in her ears, Tori looked around the group, her hands gripping one another tightly as she waited without a reply.

Shifting in his seat, Godfry continued, "I understand Agent Founder has informed you of our offer, but just to be clear I would like to take this opportunity to go over it with you again."

Godfry held up a piece of paper, waving it slightly towards her, so Tori stood and leaned forward to take it from him. They were giving her a copy of the terms in writing, just as Eli had promised. Looking down at it now, she felt her head swimming at the reality of what was happening. Her lips felt dry, and she licked them nervously as he spoke.

"As you can see, our offer is quite generous. We are willing to grant you full immunity for all actions on your part, including the assault on the orderly at the hospital, in exchange for your information and testimony against any and all parties connected to the group known as The Organization, as well as knowledge of the activities and crimes of the group previously known as the Dragons."

Tori shuddered nervously in her chair, not able to fully control the trepidation she now felt rising within her. Lifting and waving a hand slightly, she interjected, "If you please sir, could I ask a question before we go any further?"

Godfry simply nodded his approval, so she continued. "Is it my understanding then that you are wanting to clear up old cases that the Dragons may have had a part in? And, in addition to that, to lead an assault against The Organization in an attempt to destroy and or prosecute the members thereof in its entirety?"

Again Godfry nodded, "You would be correct in that understanding."

Tori could feel her conviction gaining strength, and she spoke more clearly, "Well then, I would be more than happy to give you information about the conduct and actions of the Dragons. There are a lot of people and families out there that have been touched by their acts of violence, and I am willing to do whatever I can to bring peace to those people and right those wrongs as it were."

She swallowed noticeably before she tackled the second issue, "As for information about The Organization; I can share with all of you the same information I gave to Agent Founder before, but beyond that I do not have any real information about the group itself and can only legitimately offer you a warning about them specifically."

"What kind of warning?" La Buff scoffed his tone condescending. "Are you trying to say you don't know anything about the group after all?"

"No, Sir, that is not what I am saying at all." Tori tried desperately to keep her cool. "What I am saying is, what I know is enough to get all of your men killed. The Organization is a living entity, aware of the movement of others and prepared to defend itself. I would be deeply remiss if I did not warn you about the gravity of mounting an attack against it."

"I will tell you everything I know and I am very happy that you are willing to afford me my life and chance at a future, but quite frankly after I have told you those things, I will be a dead woman. I and anyone close to me will be a target of The Organization, and there is nothing you can do to protect me from what they will do to me when they find me."

Tori paused, her chest rising and falling heavily, and she could feel her heart rate increasing further as she pushed on, "I am not concerned about myself. I have suffered a long time, and am content to be free of those who oppressed me. Who I am concerned about is this 'family' of mine that you have been searching for. I want you to stop. They are safer and happier not being found. I don't want them to know about the things that happened to me or the terrible things that I have done, and I certainly do not want them to pay the price for what I am going to share with you."

"I am also concerned about the men you will sacrifice trying to stop what cannot be stopped. Anyone you send after The Organization will be taking on a suicide mission." The room was still as everyone considered her words carefully.

After several minutes, Agent Godfry broke

the silence and stated matter-of-factly, "We appreciate your concern for the safety and wellbeing of others. However, it is the purpose of this committee to obtain the information you hold, and we are authorized to give you the terms as they are outlined in the formal agreement you now hold in your hand in exchange for it. What is to become of that information as far as how and when it is or will ever be used, is not for us or you to decide. If you are willing to provide that information, then please sign at the bottom of the page, and a copy of it will be made for your records."

Tori stared down at the page for several minutes; her eyes quickly reading over the words. When she had finished, she stood and used a pen that lay in front of Warren La Buff to sign the document and handed it back to Agent Godfry.

Her face made of stone as she moved; her heart was heavy knowing that no matter which path she chose, pain and suffering awaited someone. The page was handed to Debra, who went to make a copy of the agreement. Godfry rubbed his hands together eagerly, "Well now, I guess you may begin anytime," he indicated her chair, as if to ask her to sit and begin.

Tori's voice was monotone, "I need a map. Preferably North and South America."

Doug left the room to locate one, and while he was gone, Debra came back with Tori's copy of their agreement. she looked it over briefly, then folded it and placed it inside her jacket's inner pocket. She locked eyes with Eli and a terrible sadness overtook her.

As surely as she knew she wanted to be with him, she knew what she was about to tell would probably mean she never would be. She had much to confess, so to speak, and when she was done, she was certain he would never see her in the same way again.

X Marks the Spot

Doug was gone for several minutes, but eventually returned with a very large wall map of North and South America. Seeing the size of it, Tori reached to move the tables so that two of them stood side by side for a larger work space.

Doug had also picked up a package of colored expos, which he handed to her with a half-smile. "Thought you might like these, as well. And I grabbed the tape recorder from my desk. Thought it would be easier than trying to take notes."

Tori nodded her agreement and began to survey the map and collect her thoughts. The group took their seats around the table, but quickly realized their view was better if they stood, so the chairs were pushed back. Looking around the group, she realized this was not going to be easy, but she was going to give it her best. Her eyes met with Eli's, and he smiled, but she gave her head a single shake and began.

She started with the bush camp, marking it on the map. Then stopping to ask if anyone had a legal pad she could write on, as it helped her when she was doing tactical to make a list as she went. One was produced for her shortly, and Tori started at the top of the first bright yellow page with 'Bush Camp.' She made a list of events and main features and ended at the bottom with the words 'body count—0.'

One of the guys she had not formally met asked if there were really going to be enough bodies to count and Tori met him with a stone cold stare. She was getting into her 'special forces' aura and did not tolerate stupid questions in that mode of thought. After staring at her for a few seconds while blinking confusedly, he retracted the question with a wave of his hand as if erasing it from the air and a half-hearted "never mind."

Tori tore off the page and recorded the next stop on their journey on the next page, along with a brief description, body count—1. This time she placed a X on the map inside the circle. She continued to work up through Central America, circling, X-ing, and making notes on a legal pad until she hit El Paso, then she stopped to recap for the group.

She explained that as soon as they left the bush camp, her real training began, and Eddie used people they encountered for that purpose. Several children and women and a few men made for live targets as he began to allow her to put what she had been taught to use. Total body count for South and Central America—26.

After they entered El Paso, the trend continued as they moved across Texas, but the group became more choosey about whom they used for target practice, primarily taking homeless people and prostitutes, which would be less likely to be missed or draw attention.

When she reached the town of Scottsville, Tori paused. Circling it on the map, her mind returned to the few days they had spent holed up in a house there and the old couple that had paid for their untimely return with their lives. Debra could see this was hard for the girl, even though she did not go into any great detail about why the couple died. Tori placed two X's inside the circle for the small community. Total body count for Texas—18.

At this point, Warren La Buff stopped her, scoffing at her allegations. "You mean to tell us, you guys rode across 4000 or 5000 miles, on motorcycles, through a half dozen countries, killing 44 people, and no one even gave you a second glance?"

Tori stared at him angrily for a moment, then replied curtly, "No. It wasn't 44 people. These are the 44 people I can remember, and I am giving you details about. If you don't believe me, which obviously you don't, why don't you go check on some of the body dumps and see if they were later located to verify my story."

Grabbing the page that contained the Scottsville information, she wadded it up and threw it at him across the table. Everyone else stared in silence as La Buff reached for the page and unfolded it. He stared down at it for a moment, considering her words, and then stormed out of the room.

Tori continued across Louisiana, on into Mississippi. As she moved across, the body count began to decline per area, which was interesting to Godfry. Taking a deep breath to calm herself at again being interrupted, Tori explained that as she became more proficient at killing, Eddie saw less need for lessons and practice, so random victim numbers dropped dramatically.

She further explained that by the time they reached Florida, the number for training all but ended and they began taking jobs, which was a whole different reason and type of killing. The only people who were killed at random after the meeting in Florida were those who got in the way or posed some kind of threat to the group.

"As a side note here, one of our points of

contact for The Organization was located in Miami, Florida.." Tori threw out this extra piece of information at the moment, and others like it as she worked her way through the time line of events.

Keeping things in chronological order helped her to be organized and would hopefully give the feds more to go on when they got more into their investigation. "Of course, I was not privy to his location or actual identity; I only know that we picked up work for them several times when we were there over the years."

The conference room door opened, and Warren La Buff entered with a small stack of papers in his hand, along with the crinkled yellow page lying on top. "Wanda and Earl Blanchard," he began reading off of the police report as he rejoined the group, "Murdered at their home in Scottsville, Texas, dated almost 5 years ago, just after stepping out of their vehicle when returning from a short vacation to their daughter's house in Waco. Their bodies were found two days later lying next to their car by a neighbor who had been called by their daughter when they did not answer the phone, and she got worried. The house was a shambles, 'with every stick of furniture inside busted' and large amounts of blood found in the couple's bedroom that did not belong to anyone who could be identified. No prints or any other identifiable markings were found; no other bodies were found."

Tori dropped her head for a moment and then asked if there was a bathroom she could use. Debra led her down the hall and waited for her outside.

When they returned, an argument had erupted inside the conference room. Walking back up to the table, Tori could see that everyone had been disturbed by what she was telling them, and were even more distraught by the report that La Buff had pulled, verifying her story, at least about one of the locations of violence. Casting a stony gaze around the gathering, Tori was disgusted by their bickering, and called loudly for them to stop.

"This is what you wanted," she said in a booming voice, articulating each and every word succinctly. "You wanted to know where the bodies were buried. That is exactly what I am giving you, for as many as I can remember. What you do with that information is up to you. I have my paper in my pocket, and when I am done, I am out of here. So tell me when you have heard enough and I will stop, but until then, shut the fuck up."

"This is not fun for me. This is a detail of the five years I rode with these guys, being raped and beaten on a daily basis, on top of being made to commit such horrible and violent acts against other people. I don't want to listen to any more of your whiney ass bullshit while I am describing to you the hell from which I have escaped. Otherwise, I will just go now, thank you very much, and you all have a real nice day."

Everyone stood; jaws dropped, in stunned silence, staring at her in disbelief. They were beginning to see that Tori ran hot and cold, and was no small amount of scary when she was pissed.

Looking down at the map, they realized sadly that she had only reached the midpoint of the first year in marking, and already the body count was near 75. This was going to take a great deal of leg work and investigation to sort out after they had all the details they could get from her.

The group continued to listen on in relative quiet, only asking for clarification if it was absolutely necessary. They had lunch delivered after a couple of hours and moved to one of the empty tables for a full break while they ate. Warren La Buff made no more interruptions while they were at the map, but as soon as they sat down to eat, he started picking at her again.

Tori did not bite this time, only giving him icy stares as she pulled the meat and vegetables off her sandwich, leaving the bread on the paper. Eli watched her intently, and wished they had asked before ordering the meal for her, knowing it wouldn't amount to much without the parts she didn't like.

Walk Softly

After finishing the meal, the group moved back to the map and surveyed their progress. So far, they were up to year three, as they had been checking details periodically through police records in order to maintain some dates for their information.

Tori wished she could help them in this department, but for her, time and dates had little importance until recently. The only two times that mattered were sun rise and sun set, and the only date was the day Henry died. Eli felt a stab of pain in his heart as he wanted to console her at that moment, but he had to walk softly and did not dare break his role as Special Agent Eli Founder in front of the group.

When evening came, it was decided to order in a second meal and try to push through to the end, which they did manage at about 8 pm that night. Relieved, Tori was ready to go home with Eli and snuggle with him until the morning.

However, once it was time to leave, she was told she was not going back to the hospital, and she realized the committee as a whole did not know she had stayed at Eli's apartment the night before. "We have a place for you here," Godfry explained. "We will reconvene in the morning to iron out the final details regarding The Organization and your release."

Leaving the conference room, Tori walked obediently next to Debra as she was led to the room that would be her lodgings until she was free. It was a small room, with a bed and chair, but no other furniture in site. The bathroom was part of the room, with the sink and counter running along the far wall, and the shower and toilet that was tucked into small individual closets, one in each corner next to the sink. When she saw it, Tori thought it might be what a cell would look like.

While Tori took in the space, Debra tried to sound understanding. "I know this is difficult for you. I will be here in the morning, and we will get started early, so get a good night's sleep." With a friendly smile, she stepped outside and closed the door. Tori heard the sound of the lock. *So it is a cell.*

With another look around the room, she decided to forgo the shower and stretched out across the bed. Tori felt like she had been beaten. Eli was gone; she was almost sure of it. The haven she had found in the hospital was gone. She sighed deeply. After several minutes, she stood and moved to the corner next to the shower, behind the chair, and squatted down. Putting her right shoulder into the corner, she rested her forehead against the wall and fell asleep.

The following morning, Debra Paisley entered Tori's room ready to get to work. She had gone by Eli's apartment the night before to retrieve all of the items they had purchased for her. When she entered the small room, she did not see any sign of the girl.

"Tori," she called out, "are you in here?" She stepped over and tapped on the door that hid the toilet—no response. Turning, her eyes darted wildly looking for any sign of her, panic rising inside her throat.

Behind the chair, she noticed a shadow, slumped in the corner and exhaled a sigh of relief. As she moved towards the girl, Tori stood slowly, making her way to sit on the end of the bed.

Debra walked around so that she could look her over after having found her in such an odd place. "I have your things for you," she stated, trying to sound upbeat. However, judging by the slump of her shoulders, Tori's features were quite dark, and she was in no mood to get ready to meet with the committee.

Sitting on the bed beside her, Debra draped her arm around her new friend's shoulders, and Tori leaned against her, wanting to cry. Trying not to rush her, the older woman moved her hand up and down her charge's arm as she held the embrace, whispering that everything was going to work out.

Eventually, Tori looked up, her makeup from the day before smeared heavily. "Jump in the shower," Debra instructed her. "Put on some fresh clothes while I go down and bring up some breakfast. Then I will help you put on your makeup before the meeting."

Tori did as she was told, and while she sat on her bed waiting for the older woman to return, she sifted through her things, as they were, that had been brought over from Eli's house.

Debra returned shortly, and they ate in silence, Tori only feeling marginally better. After Debra's expert hands made quick work of the makeup, they headed down the long corridor towards the conference room for day two.

The Last Straw

Entering the conference room, Tori saw Eli sitting at the table. The rest of the committee was moving about the room discussing events of the previous day and what would need to be done next. She made her way over to where he sat and took a chair on the opposite side of the same corner, so that she was beside him, but not directly beside him. She asked in French if anyone else spoke the language or were they in private if they used it.

He gave a quick look around and informed her that French would probably not work for that purpose here. Then he laughed out loud, telling her he had missed her and could not wait for this to be over so he could take her home. His voice was quiet, not to draw attention, and his words lifted her spirits ten-fold. Tori gave him a small smile in return and hoped that it was true. The others began to make their way over to them, and it was time to begin.

Godfry led the meeting, as he usually did, and opened it by giving a brief recap of the previous day. "Thank you for the extensive list of information. We have already got people working on files for each of the locations you named, and I think what we are going to do is have the tape transcript made to work from as well."

"The map was a brilliant idea and using both, we should be able to piece together a large portion of the data with ease. That way, we will not have to keep you any longer than necessary, but bear in mind we may have to contact you or bring you in at some point in the future for confirmation or for more information on any or all of the instances you described." Tori nodded her understanding, and released a small sigh of relief that what she had given was enough.

Continuing, Godfry made a checkmark on his list of topics to address, "Now we need to discuss the specifics on The Organization. We do have Agent Founder's report on the structure, but we were hoping you would not mind giving us a recap or retelling of this flower story of yours so that we can all visualize and make the most of it." So, Tori went through the whole story again, explaining how The Organization worked, why it worked, and what occurred with Bradley Wells.

Warren La Buff was indignant when he heard what had happened to his fellow agent in detail, and Tori deduced that Eli had shortened his report in some effort to protect her. Her expression was of deep regret as she addressed La Buff and explained her feelings about the incident. "I am truly sorry about your friend. If I had been able to help him, I would have, but at that time, I was just not in any position to do so."

La Buff was outraged, gasping as he spoke,

"How could you not save him, but then you were able to kill the Dragons—all of them! I find what you say very hard to believe," he finished in an accusatory voice.

Tori sat for a moment, and then quietly asked if they wanted to hear about the night the Dragons died. "No one has asked me about that, and I guess we have reached the point it is the part you need to hear and understand most."

Everyone looked around for objections, and seeing as there was none, it was decided she should share it. Tori took a deep breath. She had told Eli that she did not want to tell her story in front of a room full of strangers, and yet she had just volunteered to do so.

Giving it a few moments of thought, Tori decided it was better to tell them a few key pieces of information first, starting with Henry. She explained that Henry had been her best friend and that after he was forbidden to touch her, they were seldom in a position to even speak to one another. When they were, those times were golden to her. The fact that he was alive, and watching over her had helped her to endure, even when things seemed their darkest.

About six or seven months before the farmhouse event, Tori and Henry had just such a period of time where they were able to speak. They had stopped at a diner, and Tori and Henry had taken seats along the window, with the others a short distance away and a bit spread out. They were traveling late at night and had the place to themselves, as they were working on a job that was going to need some planning, but it paid well and Eddie was eager to take care of it.

While the rest of the group worked on the details, Henry and Tori, who were part of the action but hardly ever part of the planning stage, sat back to back waiting.

At some point, Henry turned towards the window and asked if she could hear him. Tori was surprised, but leaned forward onto her hand with her elbow on the table as if she were overly tired. In this way, she could face the window also and replied that she could.

Henry seemed very pleased and said, "I have been working on getting you away from the Dragons, and we need this chance to talk where no one will know that the conversation has ever taken place. You understand baby girl?" Tori only nodded slightly to agree.

Quietly, he explained to her that he was going to arrange for another group to kill the Dragons and send her to live with someone who would look after her. Not understanding what he meant, she interrupted, "Why would I have to go with someone else? If the Dragons are dead, why can't I just go with you?"

He refused to explain, and simply stated, "You are going to have a different life, baby girl. A life I cannot give you. You must be strong and willing to do whatever it takes to make this happen. Promise me you will do this."

Reluctantly, Tori promised him she would do as he asked when the time came, and that was the end of the conversation. Henry got up to go to the bathroom, dropping a crumpled napkin on her table. Tori picked it up and put it in her pocket, and when she unwrapped it later, she found a small silver key. She put the key in the lining of her jacket, assuming she would need it when the time came for her new life to begin.

Less than a month later, Eddie and Henry got into a fight. Eddie was cursing at him, calling Henry a disloyal son of a bitch he should have killed years ago. They were trading blows as they fought, and as it got ugly, Tori became tempted to jump in on Henry's behalf.

As if he could read her thoughts, Red stepped up behind her and looped his arm around her waist. "You can't help him now," he spoke into the back of her head as he held her firmly, and a few minutes later, as Tori watched, Henry was dead.

They emptied his pockets and dragged his body back away from the road before riding away. They made Tori ride his bike along with them, and that night it was stripped and left where it stood the next morning. She felt like they had been looking for something specific, and thought about the key. Saying nothing, she kept it hidden and waited.

In the weeks and months that followed, Tori began to feel more and more forlorn about her life with the Dragons. She was growing exceedingly tired of being dragged around all of the time. She was tired of the road, of the jobs and of the men themselves.

All they ever wanted from her was dirty sex. The only thing they allowed her to do was to hurt and kill people. Tori missed Henry terribly and with no hope of ever having him as her friend again, she began to lose her restraint.

Eddie warned her often that she was forgetting her place, beating her regularly in the last few months. And it was true; she no longer felt the need to bow down to him and the others. Tori began to have altercations with them, and hand to hand sparing became a daily occurrence. The guys did not seem to heed its warning or take it seriously, but Tori fully intended to hurt them if she could, raw hatred now brewing inside of her. They would fight as if they were still training her, but now she had learned enough and was strong enough to win.

On one particular occasion, just a day before the farmhouse, Marcus Sanchez decided he had heard enough of Tori's backtalk and intended to do something about it. They had stopped at a secluded spot, and he was going to put her back in her place. He grabbed her by the hair, throwing her down to the ground where he intended to strip her and give her an attitude adjustment, just like the old days. Only this time, Tori was ready for him and not going down without a fight.

She made a quick dodge when he moved to grab her, knocking his hands away, rolling quickly onto her feet; she kicked him in the face and knocked him onto the ground with a savage blow to the back of his neck. The fight was short, and Marcus lay on the ground afterwards, blood pouring from his nose and gums where a tooth was missing.

Tori had never asserted herself before, but now she was a force to be reckoned with. For the first time since they had left the bush, she was allowed to sleep in peace, and no one touched her that night.

The next night, the Dragons stopped and crashed a farmhouse that appeared to be deserted, if only at the moment. As soon as they got inside, it was made clear she was expected to perform her duties as usual. Knowing that she would be able to shower and rest afterwards, she persuaded herself to give in and did her best to entertain the few that were in need that evening. *It's only a few; you can do this.* She removed her clothing and did her best to please them and put them to rest so she could have some time for herself before morning.

Of course, Red wanted a turn, and his turns always had to be special. While he was fucking her, her thoughts fell randomly, and Tori remembered the time they had been in a motel with Michael Anderson watching. She thought about him now, as Red was pulling her hair the way he did that night so long ago. She allowed herself briefly to wonder if the mysterious Michael were still alive before pushing the memory aside, *as if knowing would do you any good.*

Afterwards, she found a bathroom, where she slipped into the shower and washed away the grime of the days since she had last been able to cleanse herself. Blood oozed from her rear as she washed it, and Tori felt tired, like she couldn't go on much longer.

Henry is gone, she lamented. *There is no reason to hang on anymore.* Her new life would never come; she would always be a slave to these men, to this endless road of misery.

Standing in the bathroom drying off, Tori heard a rap on the door and opened it a crack to see it was Marcus himself, ready for a turn. Tori tried to send him away, "I'm done for the night. Maybe tomorrow, mmmk?"

He laughed at her, pushing the door open, "Naw bitch, that's not how this shit works... You're gonna do your fucking job." Closing the door behind him, he grabbed the towel she had wrapped around her and pulled her over to the sink. She had gotten away with beating him the day before, but she had never forgotten Tony's words from all those years before, *you're not gonna win. Not against all of us.*

Leaning over the sink, she relented and allowed him have his way, accepting his punishment. He was handling her roughly, pinching her and pulling her hair, then biting her ear as he held her in place. He added fresh gel to her since she had already washed the rest away, sneering as he pushing himself inside her. He emitted excited moans of pleasure while Tori fumed. *How long do I have to endure this shit? How many times do I have to be made to crawl?*

She could feel him sliding in and out of her as he flexed his hips. He was slamming against her, abusing her breasts viciously as he did so. Her rear end burned from the previous turns already taken that night and enough was enough. She had already had her shower, *god dammit*. She touched her scarred breast profusely, but it wasn't helping her calm down or remember her place.

Marcus worked her for several more minutes, squeezing her and panting. Staring at the faucet before her, Tori's clothes were piled on the sink and brushed her left hand as she gripped the edge of the basin. Her mind turning; she realized her knife was still underneath them.

Sliding her hand beneath, she whipped her arm back quickly, elbowing him in the ribs to knock him down. The pop of the blade as it extended seemed extraordinarily loud in the cramped space and she stabbed his carotid in a flash.

Blood squirted out onto her naked body, and continued to pulse over his hands as he tried to stem the flow. Falling back against the door, he sank to the floor and was dead before Tori had realized what she had even done.

Staring down at the knife in her hands, the room began to spin. She could feel the sticky blood on her fingers, and she knew the Dragons might kill her for this. Forcing down the panic, she realized the time had come. Tonight, she would bring justice to the gang of misfits, or she would die trying.

Reaching down, she pulled Marcus' body out of the way of the door. Then, she stepped back into the shower to wash his blood off her chest and to think. When she climbed out, she dried herself again, but did not bother to get dressed. She switched the light off and tip-toed out into the hall. The house was mostly dark now, as everyone had found a spot and called it a night.

Beginning in the living room, she killed each man in silence, letting his blood flow and moving to the next when his pulse had stopped. Each one was different, and yet each was the same. She looked for the most exposed major artery, and then used her knife to sever it with a quick stabbing motion.

A few she had to hold down, as they

squirmed or tried to call out after her knife found its way home. A couple were nearly decapitated by the time she finished with them. Most were drunk, and all were asleep, and that made the progress quick and easy.

It only took a few minutes to make her way through, and then all that were left was the twins. Walking lightly, Tori made it to the master bedroom, where Eddie was sprawled face down across the bed. He had not taken her that night, so although he had removed his shirt, his jeans were intact. With a quick, fluid motion she also stabbed him in the carotid, just as she had done to Marcus, then leapt onto his back and yanking his head up by his hair, cut him again from ear to ear.

As his blood spilled, Tori could see Red, who was passed out in a chair by the window in the same room. *Piece of shit.* He had started drinking as soon as he was done with her, not even bothering to get dressed. *Too bad*, Tori thought, *he might have been able to save himself and his brother if he wasn't so fucking worthless.*

Standing over him, her posterior throbbed as she looked down at his still naked body. He had passed out, lounging across a rounded stuffed chair, his legs dangling over the arm. She wanted to hurt him, to make him suffer as she had suffered so many times at his hands. This time, she picked up a large volume that was laying on the nightstand, and hit him square in the face with it, causing him to jump up with a start and fall down on his knees in anguish and surprise.

Blood poured out of his mouth and nose. He tried to call out to the others, but there was no one left to hear. Ten men had been dealt with, and he would be the one to get what he had coming to him. What they all had coming to them.

She could not risk them awakening others around them to punish them all. *You can't beat them all*; she thought, *but you can beat this one*. She hit him in the back of the head with a giant book, and he fell on his face, still resting on his knees and his ass sticking up in the air.

The yard lamp from outside shown in through the window. She looked at the way it fell across his bare naked cheeks, and she had a terribly wonderful idea.

In his drunken stupor, Red had no hope of stopping her. Tori fed her need to punish him, and stepped into the bathroom to grab the plunger. His tube of gel was still on the floor next to his pants, and she smeared it on the stick before shoving it inside of him, wanting to make sure he would take it all. He lurched forward at her action, his belly landing flat on the floor as he tried to struggle.

Dropping onto the small of his back with her knee, she held him in place as he tried to knock her off. She held her ground, grabbing the rubbery end of the device and driving it as hard as she could into his orifice. Finally, after the stick had begun to grow dark in the light that shown in the window, Tori tossed it aside. Kicking him in the side, she forced him over onto his back.

Sitting on the floor by the bathroom door was a small clothes iron that was commonly used before electricity by placing it into the hot embers of a wood fire to heat it. It now acted as a decorative door stop. Grabbing it, she cupped the body of it in the palm of her hand with the handle running over the back. Eagerly, she slapped him in the face with it, the impact causing her fingers to sting.

She liked the way it made the bones in his face crack, and as she hit him again, teeth flew out onto the floor. Suddenly, the rage inside her broke free, and she kept raising it over her head, hitting him until she could not lift her arm anymore, his lifeless body beneath her as she sat on his chest. Staring at the lump of flesh and blood that no longer resembled a human head, she dropped the iron to the floor beside him.

Standing, she went around the house in search of the bottles they had been drinking from. She finished off every one she could find, including a couple she found in a cabinet in the kitchen. When there were no more, she returned to the master bedroom, stepping over Red's body, still half afraid he would reach out and grab her, and turned on the water in the shower.

Allowing the water to wash over her, she used the shampoo to wash the blood and grey matter from her nasty hair and face. The soap smelled nice as she used it, but it brought no comfort, and she washed her nether regions, wincing in pain; afterwards she leaned against the wall, the cool tile pressed to her face, and she sobbed in ragged breaths. She stood, allowing the water to pour over her until it ran cold, then fumbling for the lever, cut off the cascade.

Awkwardly making her way out of the shower she wrapped herself in a towel and cautiously exited the bathroom, leaning on the door frame to hold herself up. Stumbling back into the bedroom, she slid down the wall next to the bathroom door. She sat staring at the bodies of Red and Eddie Farrell until the darkness overtook her, not for one second feeling sorry for what she had done to them.

Freedom Isn't Free

Tori sat in the chair, staring at her hands in silence. She could still see the blood on them, no matter how many times she washed them. Slowly, she could hear their voices as the group began to whisper amongst themselves, but her story was done. She had nothing left to say. Finally, Special Agent James Godfry called the group to order and announced it was time to discuss her future.

Tori did not look up; her face drawn with deep lines of pain no makeup could hide. Someone rested a hand on her shoulder causing her to jump. Knocking it away, she looked up and cried, "Don't touch me! Please god, don't touch me." The offender stepped back and returned to his chair obediently.

Looking around the faces of the committee, Tori sat in silence, waiting for them to pronounce judgment upon her. She deserved to be punished for what she had done. Instead, she had a piece of paper in her pocket that said she would never be indicted or prosecuted. She would be given her freedom, but freedom isn't free. It would have a price far heavier than anyone in that room could at the moment imagine.

Godfry continued to outline the decision that the committee faced next. "Tori, it is the finding of Dr. Bennet and the agreement of this committee that you are, in fact, a minor. What we must do now is to talk about your next placement."

Tori gripped the arms of the chair more firmly. *They aren't even going to let me explain why they are wrong.*

Noticing her distress, Godfry allowed the level of his voice to drop to a more compassionate tone. "We know this is not a popular topic with you and you do not agree with that finding.

However, it is what we are going to go with, and therefore we have a few options to discuss and would like your input before we make a final decision." Several around the table nodded their agreement, but Tori remained tense. "Is there anything you would like to say before we get started?"

"Why can't I stay at the hospital?" Tori blurted out immediately.

Dr. Bennet was quick to explain, "We do not feel that the hospital is benefiting you or the most appropriate place for you at this time. What you need is social interaction—normal social interactions—with people." After a quick pause, he laid out the options. "You see, we just don't think you are getting the personal attention you need in that environment. Instead, we would like to consider two other options."

"Because of your age, we thought it might be appropriate to place you into a foster care situation. That way you could get more of a feel of what it is like to be part of a family unit. If we are able to place you soon, we have a family with two teenage boys that would be willing to have you. You would be able to attend High School and live the life of an average teenager."

He stopped for a moment to allow her to consider what the foster family would be like and have to offer her, and she was beginning to shake her head in disgust...*un-fucking believable.*

"However," he then continued, "you scored very well on the educational testing, and we do appreciate your doing your best, by the way, and so it has been suggested that you would be better served in a more adult role or capacity. For example, you could reside in a halfway house where you would be able to hold a job, learn financial responsibility, and still have the interaction of a small group environment. This path would lead you more quickly into being able to attend a college or university if you so choose."

Tori sat clenching and unclenching her jaw for several seconds, looking from face to face. The only one who was easy to read was Warren La Buff, and that was because his squinty eyes and the stiff way he held himself made his displeasure at the entire situation unmistakable.

The rest of the group looked at her, hands in their laps, like they could wait all day for her response without giving away an ounce of how they felt about it. Finally, Eli smiled, and asked if she had any questions or comments on the subject. *He really shouldn't have done that.*

"Any comments?" Tori's voice started low. "Well, I am glad to see you are all so concerned about me getting out into the 'real' world for some 'normal' social interaction." She could feel the anger bubbling inside of her. "And I really only have one question. What am I supposed to do when I get there?" She began to move her hands like a little puppet show, punctuating her sentences and illustrating her words.

"You know, I saw a school once. Had all these little kids out on the playground, running around screaming and laughing, and I realized how different I was from them. I never went toschool. Never even talked to a little kid, or laughed or played with anyone my size. What am I gonna do in a foster home, hanging out with a bunch of wet behind the ears kids? Talk about sex and drugs and how a 5th is good for dulling pain? There's some life lessons for you. I bet their parents will appreciate my sharing that one."

"How about, I show them how to run wire and lay charges? Do they have any small structures they would like removed?" A few of the listeners began to shift uncomfortably as she mocked them. "How about, how to clean an SR-25? I could take them out for some target practice, show them what I am really good at. Any chance I could get my knife back?" Her voice had been making a slow, steady climb and was reaching its peak, "Are you people out of your god damned minds?"

"So is that what you are afraid of, hurting someone?" Eli's voice was quiet and calm.

"Afraid of? I'm not afraid of anything," Tori rolled on, fully charged. "I know who I am and what I can do, and it's nothing I want to share. What do you think; I can just get that time back? I can't ever be one of those kids. I will never have what they have, the memories, the experiences, and I thank god they don't have mine. I will never be one of them. Never." Tori trembled with rage.

"So you would like to get a job and live with adults then." Godfry stated flatly.

"I don't want to live with anyone." Eli looked like he had been slapped, but Tori took a deep breath, gearing up for the second wave. "Adults would be worse than kids. Adults judge you when they don't even know you. They look at you and see things, like the scar on your face, and don't say anything or speak to you. They smile fake smiles and worm around the truth being 'polite'. They watch people do horrific things, and never stand up and defend the weak. Or they are the ones hurting the weak, beating and biting and burning."

She stopped cold, suddenly hitting the end of what she had to say. "You send me where you want," she spit out the words as she stood and headed for the door. Out in the hall, she flopped down on the bench outside and pushed her face into her hands. She wanted to cry, but tears are for the weak, so she just sat there, breathing into her palms and waiting.

Some minutes later, Eli came out and sat down next to her, leaning back against the wall. Taking in a deep breath, he let it escape slowly before he spoke. "OK, so here's the deal." He kept his voice as even as he could. "You are going to a halfway house in a couple of days. After you have been there six months, the committee will reconvene with you, and if everything has gone well, you will be released for good. Basically, what we call emancipated, because even though we are not for certain how old you are, they still suspect you are a minor at this time. Also, it will give us a little more time to locate your family. If we haven't found them by then, we probably aren't going to."

Tori thought for a moment then lifted her head, "So there is no other way to get through this? I mean; I don't have a choice, I have to do this?"

"Yes," Eli spoke softly, trying to stick to the plan, "You have to do this. But, after the 6 months you can go where ever you want and live, however, you want. So if you want to be alone, just make it through and you can do that." In the back of his mind, Eli still hoped she would return to him and share his little apartment.

"Ok, well, I don't want you to find my family. I want them to stay safe and hidden, untouchable by the people I have betrayed." Tori swung her gaze to stare him in the eye.

"As far as your family goes, they are going to try and identify you, whether you want them to or not." He gave a small shrug, wishing he could do more. "It's not my call, and I don't think it's the committee's call on that one."

Tori sighed deeply. "And what if things don't go well? If I fuck up when I am in this half-way house, what happens then?"

Eli looked down at his hands, folded in his lap. "You may have to stay longer or we will do something else. The point is, you have to try."

"Do I still have to do all this other stuff? Go to group meetings and talk to the doctor and you and all of that shit?" her head still turned to look at him, she could see him swallow hard, not meeting her gaze.

"You won't really have any meetings or anything like that, and I will not be coming to visit you." Eli looked like he had been kicked. "I will not see you again after today until we have the meeting at the end of the six months' time. I can't say I will be happy about that; I mean it's only been about a month since I even heard of you... but I am going to miss you."

Tori felt a stab of sadness, and realized he was truly someone she could trust, so she asked in a much softer tone, "Is this what you think is best for me or what they think is best for me? If you tell me to go because you want me to, I will."

"I don't want you to go!" Eli's voice cracked, and he drew a deep breath and held it before continuing. "What I mean is, I don't want you to go, but I know it is what is best for you. I am just afraid that this is goodbye, and I am really not ready to tell you goodbye. I told you that my spare room is yours, and I would never go back on my word—it will be waiting for your return."

The door opened, and Debra stepped out. "I need to take her back to her room," she informed

Eli quietly.

Even though she did not know any details about their relationship, Debra understood how hard this was going to be on the both of them. Tori gave Eli a quick kiss on the lips, then stood to follow Debra down the hall. Watching the floor as she walked, neither of them spoke until they were back inside the small chamber.

"Don't give up," Debra said reassuringly. "If things are meant to work out between you and Eli, they will." Tori looked surprised she was familiar with the couple's plight, but Debra just gave a knowing smile. "For now, I need to tell you a little bit about where you are going. We need to get your clothes and everything together today. Tomorrow, we have to take care of any loose ends early, because your plane leaves at 2 pm. That will put you in LA at about 4 pm."

"LA?" Tori interrupted, "You guys are sending me to LA?" She was suddenly overtaken by conflicting visions of LA and leaving Eli.

"Yes, we are," Debra smiled broadly at her

surprise. "It makes sense for logistical reasons, and we have a retired agent there who is going to be giving you a job and helping you out, basically. He runs a music store and builds custom guitars. He could use a little help, so it is a nice fit for him since you already play. Plus, he owes Jim a favor, which Jim is cashing in on for you."

"Well, now, I don't know if I want anyone using up favors just for me," Tori started to protest, but deep down she was already hooked *a music store!* Although it had been a few years since she had touched a guitar, playing was the one thing other than alcohol that made her feel good. Henry was the one who had taught her to play, so that made it even dearer to her.

After hearing where she was going, she was suddenly eager to get on with it. Besides, Eli had promised he would be waiting for her return in six months, and that was something very good to look forward to. A smidge of fear tickled the back of Tori's mind, but she did her best to push it away. It was the fear of good things happening, because they, sooner or later, would lead to something bad.

Debra told Tori someone would bring dinner by to her in a little while, and for her to go ahead and pack up her things in the suitcase Eli had delivered if she wanted. Finally, she told her she would see her in the morning and let herself out before locking the door behind her. Tori sat in the silence after she left, not really sure if she were happy or sad. So many things were happening at once; so many things left to come.

Standing up, she picked up the suitcase and let it fall open onto the bed. Inside was the book of German fairy tales Eli had given her. The last time she had seen it, she had left it lying on the floor next to her bed back at the hospital. *He must have gone back and gotten it for me;* she thought, and as she cracked it open, a broad smile crossed her face as she read the note he had penned inside.

About the Author

Anyone who knows me could tell you, I am a friendly kind of person, never met a stranger and take up conversations any where at any time. I work hard, and my mind never seems to shut down, as I wake up often in the middle of the night with ideas pouring out and demanding to be dealt with. Of course that means much of my books were written in the middle of the night.

I grew up and still live in the great state of Texas where everything is bigger, where we have warm weather and a central location. I love my state, my town, and my family, which includes my four sons, my significant other, and many friends as well.

I have thoroughly enjoyed writing the books that are currently available and hope you will enjoy reading them just as much. And of course, there will be many more stories to come.

Sneak Peek of Bound

Book 2 in A New Life Series

Now Available

Prologue

Special Agent Eli Founder sat on his bed, staring at the small volume of German Fairytales. He had retrieved it from the hospital for her, and intended to place it inside the suitcase with her belongings, a special message penned on the first few pages.

The problem was; he had been about the task for over an hour and was still torn with what he should write. The girl had moved him in a way he had never expected, and although he could admit to himself that their relationship would more than likely end, it hurt. He wanted the chance to let it play out, regardless of where it led. He wanted the chance to love her. Most of all, he wanted to cling to the possibility that they would have more time.

Running his fingers through his coal black hair, he spoke out loud, despite the fact that he was alone in the apartment. "You better suck it up, big boy. In the end, this comes down to one thing. You've still got a job to do. And so does she..." His voice trailed away and he pulled the cap off of the felt tipped pen, scrawling in clean cursive:

My Dearest Tori,

I know the past was filled with difficult times, and your future feels uncertain. Understand that you are not alone in your quest and that even though your path will not be an easy one, you are strong, and you will endure, so long as you endeavor to persevere. My thoughts and hopes are with you.

Yours Always,

Eli

Printed in Great Britain
by Amazon.co.uk, Ltd.,
Marston Gate.